THE RAVEN'S LAST BET

A DUET OF BELLES

DARING BELLES
BOOK ONE

CERISE DELAND

THE RAVEN'S LAST BET

BY CERISE DELAND

THE RAVEN'S LAST BET

BY CERISE DELAND

*First published with a talented group of Regency authors in the connected anthology, **The Wedding Wager**, this story is a novella starring lovers who have never had the stars aligned in their favor...until now! Enjoy!*

CHAPTER 1

25 Royal Crescent
Bath, England

"*I* won't do it," Henry Seymour Wallace told his father.

It's one thing to return home after six years fighting the enemies of Britannia in India and Spain and be told one must don leg shackles, but quite another when one is given a time limit, a purse as compensation—and a prize most elusive and alluring.

"I won't." Harry stood firm in his sire's library and felt the frigid blast of the older man's disapproval deep in his bones. His gimpy leg ached and he longed to sit, but he'd be damned if he would.

"That's absurd, boy." His father pushed up his thick glasses and peered toward him.

Harry, who'd been addressed as "Colonel, sir," for nigh

onto two years, moved not a muscle at the prick of his father's diminutive 'boy.'

His father's rheumy gaze softened. Harry knew his father could only detect the blur of his outline. "I've made the promise, Harry. The date. Signed the papers. The marriage will be. I've no time to dally. Nor do you."

Harry's circumstances bore that out. One did not become one's father's heir—a duke's heir, at that—and not feel the pinch. But the sudden death of Harry's older brother George last month (a kind fellow who had excelled unfortunately at keeping too many mistresses and siring an illegitimate child) had precipitated this state of affairs. That, coupled with his own injury, had cut short his tenure in His Majesty's cavalry.

Oh, he was grateful to have loving parents to return to and comfort. However, to arrive home only to deal not only with George's recent demise and news of great debts, but to hear his father's order to marry in all haste, made Harry more unsteady on his feet.

He dug his new ivory-tipped cane into the pale pink and azure Aubusson carpet to which he had been summarily called."I need a respite, Father. George's death and revelations of his financial obligations are a blow. Let alone news of his child and two mistresses. I arrived home only—"

"Yesterday." The man rapped his fingers on his broad walnut desk, the pulse of it ringing in Harry's ears like death knells. "It's enough."

"To assume George's role as steward of the estates? To deal with the mountain of debts he incurred to gaming hells and this woman who bore his child? No, sir. I am barely familiar with all the facts of his poor finances. Indeed, I am astonished at his profligacy. How many mistresses does a man need? Are we certain he had only two?"

"I wish I could say, Harry. Honestly, I do." His father shrugged, pushed his thick glasses up his nose and with his frown, conceded momentarily. "I know it is overwhelming. If I were capable, I would deal with it all. But you know that is not so."

His father's eyesight had never been good. For years before George came of age to assume many of the duchy's affairs, their mother had read documents to their father. His father had employed an estate agent who had, until that man's death ten years ago, been the guiding light of the Meredith estate prosperity. George had assumed many of the former manager's duties. To good outcome too, or so he had always told the duke. But now that George was gone, too, the family saw the records and understood how George had misused the truth.

"There is only one cure for it all. You. You, Harry. You must right us. I have never been overdrawn with our bank. Never been in arrears to our creditors. Never wished to see our name tarnished with unpaid invoices to dress shops and milliners. Nor to women who..." The Duke of Meredith cleared his throat, then turned his face toward the light of the window and the rolling hill down to the middle of Bath. "Nor to women who have been associated with our family."

One of whom has born my brother a child who will never have a father. Nor, it seems, means to have an education or even food upon the table.

Harry sighed. "I promise, sir, to do the best I can as quickly as I can. By all of them, too. But as to this marriage business, that cannot be."

"I insist. You know the girl."

"She is no longer a girl, sir." *Besides, she was always older than her years. She'll blister her father's ears with objections. And me? Burn me at the stake.*

His father waved away his objection. "You knew her when young. You fancied her, too."

"She was sixteen, Your Grace. I was eighteen." *She was*

7

considered beneath my rank then, and you disapproved. Then sent me away.

If his father's failing blue eyes could have truly met his, they would have pierced his with the older fellow's fierce intent. "She's eight years older now. And ripe to be wed. With all the talk of this marriage wager between Lady Pandora Osborne and Lady Octavia Sewell the comely females will soon be gone. Miss Sara Fleming included. Even if she has failed to make up her mind about any man, this year some blade will snap her up."

"What?" His father spoke in riddles. "Who are these two women...? And a wedding wager? I don't understand."

"These ladies, cousins competing for tiaras and such, have made a bet with each other to get unmarriageable women wed quickly. It doesn't concern you except that their efforts mean many young women will soon be off the marriage mart. Your girl included. You must act quickly not only because of that but because our family reputation demands you correct what George hath wrought."

Harry shook his head. "Unbelievable."

"Not really. Your girl is considered one of the unacceptable ones that the two women vow to marry off."

Unacceptable? She's a beauty Helen of Troy would envy. "Sara Fleming is no chattel."

"Indeed, she is not." His father chuckled. "Though since you've been abroad, she has become rather... hmmm...notorious."

"Notorious?" Harry did not believe that. Sara had written to him about how she refused two men's proposals. That did not constitute a tarnish of her reputation. Nor had she indicated that she'd acted inappropriately with either man. *The only man she'd ever kissed was me.* "You think she's ruined?"

"No, not ruined, Harry. Not in the sense of...violated."

His father wiped a hand across his mouth. "But she did accept the proposals of two gentlemen in the past few years."

"Accepted them?" How could that be? Sara had never written him that she'd wed. Nor had his mother who was always full of news of the Fleming family. "Both? How?"

"That's just it. She agreed to wed. Both times. But as soon as she got to the altar, she ran."

"Dear god." Harry hooted. "Sara was always fleet of foot."

His father scowled at him, a look that warned him of a battle stirring. One he did not wish to fight. For he would lose, as ever he had with the man.

He leaned upon his cane and sought a way to halt his father's advance upon him. "Explain to me what you mean about her running. If her father had accepted both proposals…?"

"One at a time, Harry. One at a time, he signed the papers for her dowry and her marriage benefit, too. All was put in readiness. The vicar, the church, the wedding breakfast, her gown, all decided and times set. And then…" His father snapped his fingers. "She appeared at the church door, paused, then turned and ran."

Relief sang through him. *So she had never married.* It was insanity that he cared. "Amazing."

"Not as amazing as the sums her father has had to pay to the two deserted bridegrooms."

Harry winced. "Set her poor father back, did she?"

"To the tune of thousands."

"Tragic."

"Silly, if you ask me. But then, 'poor' Dashiell Fleming is rich as Midas."

"And now you turn that to your advantage?" Harry could not quell his outrage at his father's actions.

"And yours, son."

"No, sir. Far from it."

9

"There are many advantages, Harry. You wished to marry her before you left for Spain. Tell me now you don't want her?"

"Years ago I would have snatched her up and carried her away to Scotland if you hadn't stopped me! Now? I don't know her! God's breath, Papa! Six years is a long time. I am... hardened." *Brittle. Riddled with headaches. Nightmares. A feeble leg.*

"But she, my boy, is even lovelier than before. A sprite in her youth. At twenty-four, she is," he said and waved a hand, "Venus on the half-shell."

"Her looks," Harry said as he recalled her radiance with a flash of need, "were always appealing."

"To more than you, son. Today, she is stunning and yet she has this growing reputation that threatens not to embellish her aura, but tarnish it. Her father fears for her future."

"While you, in need of ready funds to meet the demands of George's paramour, fear for mine?"

"Our future, Harry. Ours."

"Thus, you have made this bargain with him to seal her fate and mine. Not wise, sir."

"I love you, Harry. Admire your fortitude in battle. Applaud your success to rise in the ranks. Rejoice with you in your triumphs. I have your happiness in mind when I do this. So, too, does Dashiell Fleming take Sara's in hand. He loves his oldest daughter with a madness. But make no mistake, he fears if she does not wed soon and to one he chooses, she'll impoverish him. The man she weds should and can be you. Dashiell and I have agreed."

Harry stood at attention. "*That* is the problem, Papa."

His father, weary, shook his head.

Harry scoffed. "What makes you think *Sara* will agree? Furthermore, what on earth made you think *I* will?"

The once dashing fellow got a twinkle in his milky eyes. "One glance at her, and you will not be able to resist."

"Papa, I am no green boy. I've been away among men who've shared what they know about love and lust. And even though I have taken no mistresses, I do have experience—"

His father thrust up a hand. "Thank heavens."

Harry sighed, remembering how infatuated he'd been with Sara...and how long it took him to accept that they were no more than childhood friends and correspondents. "I have met in my travels a few comely women."

"Not like this, my boy."

"Oh, she cannot be that lovely." Even as he said it, he took bad odds he was very wrong. She'd been a bright angel at four. A scamp at six. A bloody terror at ten. A jaw-dropping beauty at fourteen. No wonder men had proposed. Wanted her. With the golden waterfall of her hair, those flashing jade eyes...and all her father's money.

What was there not to like?

At a draw in their argument, he would show his father he'd win. "I will go to her tomorrow and tell her I refuse to do this."

"Do as you wish. It will not cancel the agreement."

"Have you received the funds?"

"Next week, at the earliest, so say my bankers."

"I see." There was time, but Harry knew not what to do with it. He grew livid, his heart pounding as it did just before an assault on the enemy. "How much?"

The sum beggared his imagination.

26 Royal Crescent
Bath, England

Fury burned a hot trail up Miss Sara Fleming's spine. Her

hands shook with rage as she stepped toward the sconce and read the story in the gossip sheet a second time.

How could someone print something so absurd?

'We have it on good authority that a wedding date is set for a certain Miss F— and the new heir to the great dukedom of M—. This time, the young lady cannot refuse. Her father, that gentleman who brews the ambrosia we consume every day, has purchased her groom before she can run down the aisle. A fine solution to her propensity to accept too many proposals, don't you agree, Dear Reader?'

She'd never marry anyone who took money for the privilege. Not even him! Especially him! And how could he have agreed to such a travesty? He'd never been one to bow to machinations of the *ton*? And his father was no tyrant. Nor was her own. This was an outrage.

"Lies! All lies!"

Anger had her swaying on her feet. This had to be a rumor. A bad one. A vicious one.

Only her father could confirm it.

She caught up the skirts of her dressing gown with her good hand and whirled toward her door.

"Go to bed, Mary." Her maid had no need to wait until she'd resolved this problem. Papa would be enraged…if the story was false. Or if it was true, he could be pig-headed. Then she'd be awhile.

She hurried down the hall toward her father's sitting room. Just after midnight and he'd still be awake nursing his brandy and his latest book.

She stood before his door. Logic was the manner in which to proceed. Haste and red hot argument never made progress with the man who had single-handedly built a fortune in whisky in twenty-eight years. That he had spent too much love and money on his oldest daughter's cold feet was his liability…and Sara knew it all too well.

She knocked.

And marshaled her points.

She had always had choices. Papa had encouraged her in that, as in all else. Studying Latin and French diligently, buying novels she wished to read, understanding the proportions of Palladio and Adam, she had enjoyed her youth. If she also found that most men in her circle had never mastered the art of conversation, she tolerated them for the minutes the *ton* required by etiquette. Then she moved on to those males who had a sprig of sense (most of them older, by the bye) and had wit to spare.

Her Papa was the man who served as her model. Another was Papa's younger brother, Alfred. Of course, her own mama had been the very one to encourage her to find a husband whose conversation would amuse as well as inspire. Regrettable that Mama was not here to see so few met Sara's standards. Useful that Sara was responsible for steering her younger sister in the ways of the marriage mart.

Meanwhile she herself was confronted with this outlandish story that her Papa had a plan to marry her off and had told the world she would end her spinsterhood in the most shameful manner.

She corrected her posture, rapped on his door and inhaled.

Forthwith, his heavy foot fall approached. He flung open the door to her. One glance at the newsprint in her hand and he nodded and stepped aside. Positioning himself before the alabaster fireplace which in the August heat was bare, he loomed like the beautiful dark angel he was. Silver-haired, grey-eyed and broad-shouldered, Mister Dashiell Howard Fleming was a determined man few ever countered.

All she had to do was raise the gossip rag in her right hand and cock her head in question.

"It's time for you to marry, Sara."

13

"This is not like you!" She hurled the news sheet to his feet. "I won't do it."

"You will."

"No."

"Very well, Sara. I must say it, eh? You have your sister to consider."

"Millicent does quite well. Men fill her dance card and ask for the supper dances." Sara saw the evidence of it each day and night as she accompanied the exquisite eighteen-year-old blonde to every tea, soiree and ball. "They find her lovely. Charming."

"And tarnished by her sister's failures to secure a match."

"Who would dare say that?" She'd challenge them to a duel. Win, too!

"I understand the reasoning of the upper classes, my dear."

"But you have heard Millie at table. She's found no man yet who's caught her fancy."

"A good thing. But she's been out since June in London and received no offers."

She huffed. "You don't want to hand her off to just any fellow. I know you don't, Papa. So why be so insistent that she do it quickly?"

He inhaled and stared at her with hard truths glittering in his eyes. "Because that story in the Bath *Gazette* is only a fraction of those circulating about you. I should not have agreed to allow you to go out with her."

Sara gasped, but stood her ground. "You are not ashamed of me. I—I know you aren't. You love me and said you would send me as Millie's chaperone to show the *ton* you were proud of me. I have always known the reason you rescued me from the blunder of marrying those other two is that you love me."

"I do, my darling child. But you must admit you know the reason this state of affairs must end."

She fought hot tears along with her pride, but would admit nothing.

"Not only is it outrageous that you as the eldest and unmarried are allowed to go out as chaperone to your sister, but also that now many men may think it possible to court Millicent and propose in the hope she too will run."

"No, no." Yet it was possible. Probable. Hateful. *Didn't people do dreadful crimes for want of money? Why not propose to any innocent young woman and hope to make a windfall?* "They wouldn't."

"They could, Sara. Not only to Millicent now, but you as well. Once more."

"Well, I won't accept any man! You shan't pay anyone else for me bolting!"

"I agree. That's why you will marry Harry." He nodded toward the foolscap on the carpet.

"Is it all true then?" She saw the admission in his sparkling eyes.

"The duke agrees."

Sara stomped her foot.

He cast her a warning look.

"Yes, I am angry. You would be too if someone arranged your marriage." Her parents' union had been a love match. That it was also the marriage of one whisky distiller to another made it a sublime one. "You and Mama always preached that Millie and I find men we adore."

"You did once fancy Harry."

"Ohhh, that was so long ago." *He does not want me now. If he had, he would have given me some indication in his letters how he cared. But there was not a word. Nary a hint of anything more than a confluence of sentiments.* "With George gone, Harry's to be the next duke. If he was above my touch six years ago, he flies above the clouds now."

"I never agreed that he was beyond you."

That was Meredith who refused. "Of course not. You are a self-made man who would never agree that a fellow who inherited his wealth holds a candle to you." She stepped nearer to her father, the moonlight through the far windows highlighting his fine chiseled features. "His Grace opposed the union then. Why now?"

"His Grace agrees this is best for all of us."

She flapped her arms. "But does *Harry* agree? Dear me, Papa. He's only just home from France. I saw him alight from his carriage yesterday morning." *He looked...older. Fit. His soft brown hair, shaggy. His uniform dashing, dusty and stained.* "Well? Does Harry want this?" *Me?*

Her father remained silent.

"I see." She narrowed her eyes at him and took a step toward him. She had to know how the earth had suddenly spun in the opposite direction. "Why is it best for the house of Meredith to marry into a family of trade? I wonder... Because the Duke of Meredith feels the sting of his oldest son's sins? Or...or he has debts to pay? Big ones. *Oh, my.* That's it. Isn't it? What a kettle of fish. Poor Harry. Sold to the merchant's daughter."

"He cared for you when you were younger."

And I never stopped caring for him. That's why those others paled in comparison. But I'll never marry a man, no matter who he is, if he's been purchased for me! "He did. Yes, but I am older, no coy girl. And war changes a man. Look at Cousin Wilfred. Home nearly a year and the man still suffers a palsy that rattles his teeth. Screams at the sound of thunder."

"I have it on good authority from His Grace that his second son is of sound mind and body."

Harry's body did appear to be more than merely sound. He looked delectably muscular, if weary to his bones.

She shook off the vision of him wounded, hurt, in need of solace and a kind hand to help him. "I won't do it."

"It is arranged. The legal documents signed. The vicar, the breakfast here, of course."

She winced. How could that be? She picked at her knowledge of the rules of the Church and State about marriage.

"Imagine, my dear." Her Papa crushed her confusion with his haste. "You will become the Countess of Ravensford. One day you will be a duchess. Marry him. The only way."

He stepped from the fireplace, his arms out toward her to enfold her in his care.

He was a burly man, broad in the chest, big of heart, stout of character, and she adored him. Her cheek to the cool brocade of his banyan, she welcomed his solace.

But she would find a way to defy him.

She must.

CHAPTER 2

*S*ara winced hearing the clanging of pots and pans in the scullery. With her back flat to the wall, she closed her eyes and concentrated on listening for the moment when the maid would finish her chores and go to her bed in the far kitchen alcove.

She'd almost given up hope of escape when the maid, muttering to herself, finally declared her independence from her drudgery and shuffled off to her pallet.

Sara took the last two steps down the servants' stairs to the door to the kitchen garden. Out and around the fencing, she headed for the kitchen door in the house next to theirs. She grasped the knob, turned and rushed inside. The butler at the Meredith place was an elderly fellow, Briggs by name. He trusted far too many too often. Luckily few in town knew of the man's penchant to leave such a distinguished abode open to the world.

"And to me," she murmured as she closed the door behind her with careful attention that the latch clicked most quietly. Then up the back stairs she ran, two steps—indelicately—at a time. Haste was of the order.

She knew where she hurried—and hoped to heavens she'd not roust Harry from his bed.

She had overheard at the Assembly Room ball tonight that Harry was expected. She'd not seen him. Truly, she had looked. The search for him to play, to spar, to torment each other was her practice, born in childhood, continued until he went away to India. Indeed, she'd always looked for him everywhere. Her earliest memories were of him, laughing at her, with her, teaching her how to swim. Him on the green, his wooden sword in hand. Had he been eight? She, six? And he carved her a sword from a fallen tree branch, then commanded her to be *en garde*. Oh, yes. He'd also been the one who taught her best how to ride a horse.

Harry and his bets that he would win at everything. Cards, Chess. Duels. Racing. At first she'd been foolish to challenge him, but she had. Never winning, either, until she gained command of her limbs and her instincts, and began to win against him. Was she fourteen? Fifteen, most like. He'd been shocked but then, proud of her.

She'd admired him. His largesse. His chivalry to graciously lose to her. She had pictures of him in her mind so hazy, so indelible that she knew not the real from the fantasy of Harry, her friend. Her torment. Dashing, laughing, beyond her touch, Harry, the duke's second son.

She'd wanted to see him tonight. In the brilliance of a glittering ballroom. As candlelight burnished his chestnut hair with the fires of autumn. As he caught sight of her, his friend. As his lips spread wide in welcome and greeted her with the recognition of their friendship—and never anything more.

But he had not appeared. She understood why. He would need rest from his long journey home from the Continent. Or time to mourn his older brother's loss with his father. Instead, she would confront him with their mutual problem.

Unforeseen. Life-changing because if they did not fight it, they were to be more than they had ever been to each other. If their fathers had their way, Harry and she would be one. How that revolution in the duke's thinking turned on money, she did not know specifics. Why her father thought it prudent, she'd understood but did not believe he could remain so stubborn. Because before she'd seen the news in the local *Gazette* of her impending marriage to her age-old friend and next door neighbor, Harry would never be more to her than an acquaintance from childhood. Never her bridegroom.

She scoffed at the word as she made it to the third floor. She knew his door, second from the stairs. Recalled it from the time she'd sneaked into his rooms when she'd been eight... Or was it nine?

She knocked softly. Twice.

He did not answer.

She raised her hand ready to rap again when the door swung wide and...and...oh, my, he took her breath away.

He was naked. Sun-browned skin in such expanse filled her eyes. His broad bare chest dusted with soft brown hair had her gasping. She tore her gaze upward to a strong throat, wide jaw and a smile that welcomed her to him. For the first time in long years, she felt the warmth of his aura, his presence in her life the very comfort she had so long missed and for which she had, with remorse for his absence, yearned.

Her gaze flickered downward, his corded arms open in hearty invitation to enter into his embrace. And yes, *yes*, he did wear breeches that molded well to the power of his thighs. A clasp of friendship would be permissible. Brief, too. His arms, appealing as they appeared, were not where she should be, scantily clothed as she was. And he too. But she went to him, her cheek to the smooth strong planes of his chest.

Far too soon, she pulled back and offered her cheek.

He hooted and pecked her there. "I expected you earlier."

"Clearly," she observed, then waggled a finger at his marvelously sculpted ribs. "Have you a banyan?"

He shrugged. The rogue. "It's hot."

She feigned reproach.

Nonchalant, he leered at her. That white flash of teeth told her he knew too damn much about her flaunting of rules. His green-brown eyes declared it as they skipped down her dressing gown. "You, my girl, are not in formal attire, either."

"Oh, forget formalities." She backed her way in.

He followed her, his gaze eating up her face and form as if she were a sweetmeat he desired. *As if that were true.*

He made no move to don a shirt. Nor should she have asked it of him. She preferred him as he was, bare to her. In many ways, Harry Wallace had always been bare to her. Better so now that they had this problem to solve together.

"We must talk, Harry. The sooner we end this charade, the better."

"Why?" He slid the tip of one finger down the column of her throat to her bare shoulder. Lifting a long length of her unbound hair, he grasped it and caressed the strands.

She swatted his hand away lest he feel how her skin quivered at his touch.

He looked at her askance, as if to warn her not to stop him. "I rather like the possibilities."

"No, you don't!" Earthy as ever, he could destroy her attempt to apply logic. Worse, the fragrance of his citrus and sandalwood cologne tickled her nostrils. She pushed the appeal away, determined to get past the childish infatuation.

"I've been away a long time and my father's orders stick in my craw. Your's too, I bet." He strode away, good enough to close the door upon them, but then, he crossed his arms and leaned back against the portal. She suddenly had the very new impression she was a mouse offered cheese by a very big unpredictable cat. "One o'clock in the morning, however, is not the most conducive time to discuss this."

"Why not?" She did like the hour, given his attire...or rather lack thereof. More men should wear less. It would give women a proper estimate of the goods they might acquire by marriage. Men were always so buttoned up. Unlike ladies who were required by fashion to display more skin than sense. In Harry's case now, this particular lady could view the rigid lattice of his ribs and the fine V that marked the line from his waist downward beneath his trousers toward his groin and his...hmmm, rather appealing...unmentionables.

"Look up here, my girl."

She blew out a gust of air as her gaze met his. "Really, Harry. I know what you've got there."

He chuckled. "Once. When you were twelve, you did. Now? No. *Things*, my dear, have changed."

She felt the fire of how she blushed to the roots of her hair. "Fie on you, Harry Seymour Wallace. I am here to solve this problem."

"I have only just learned of it today, Sara."

"As did I less than an hour ago!"

"Notable that you've come so soon armed for battle. But as for me," he said as if he spoke of today's weather, "I have not yet marshaled all my objections to the plan." His luminous hazel gaze traveled from her lips down her chest to the ribbons of her dressing gown tied at her cleavage.

She ignored his perusal, even if her blossoming breasts did not. "Well, I've thought of it. But really, what is there to say except you won't do it?"

He inhaled and pursed his lips. They were lush for a man. Sensuous. She recalled how they had probed and lured when she was sixteen and she had insisted he kiss her a second time. He had, and her breasts had…

She cleared her throat, then spun away to flounce into the far wing chair. "Give me a brandy, why don't you? We'll toast your homecoming. We should. I should. I want to."

"Thank you." He gave her one of his lop-sided smiles that transformed his appearance from gentleman to something harsher…more menacing. Then he did as she bid and strolled to his sideboard, unstoppered his brandy decanter and poured two generous draughts into snifters.

It had been so many years since she'd seen him, truly seen him, that she reveled in the sight of the dashing male animal he'd become. When he'd left home six years ago, he'd been a long, lean youth. Fleet of foot, quick to laugh, hard to anger, swift to forgive, he was a man she had admired for his ready wit. Now he might still claim all those abilities, but he had the gravitas of an older man, prematurely wise from rigors of the battlefield.

"To you," he said as he handed her a glass and lifted his own. "The woman of the hour."

"I drink to you, sir. The man home from the wars. The new earl." She touched her crystal snifter to his and took a hearty draft of the luscious smoky stuff. "My condolences on the loss of your brother, George. I liked him. He was always chipper. A family trait, I think."

He downed a good swallow of his brandy and considered the far wall. "Up for a lark. A jokester. A fast friend who would give you his shirt, his last penny. A huge loss for us all. My mother is inconsolable."

"Still in the country, is she?" Sara loved his mother. Having lost her own nine years ago, she valued those women who'd been her mother's friends. The duchess had a hearty wit that many in town disparaged. Society criticized her for her friendship with Sara's mother, a *cit*, even if she was a rich one. Sara hated to see what the *ton* would do to the Merediths and to her father, his business and Millicent, if the duke welcomed Sara to his fold.

"I go down early tomorrow to see my mother, then return here the next day to attend to the legal matters." He sat opposite her in the matching Chippendale.

"And this marriage proposal. I assume you have told your father how impossible it is."

"I have."

"And?"

"He will not reneg."

At that, she took another drink. "You must convince him."

Harry sat back and considered her for a long minute with sad eyes. "Papa tells me you've made a challenge for yourself by jilting a few fellows."

"My father backed my decisions."

"Good man," Harry said and she was happy for his praise.

"He is. But now, in this, he is most adamant. I cannot let him dictate to me, or to you, either."

"Why haven't you found a man you like, Sara?"

"What kind of question is that?" She fought with herself at how shrewish she sounded. But a bother, she would be. "Why haven't you found a woman you like?"

He lifted his empty glass and held it up to the light from the candles in the wall sconce. "I've been preoccupied."

She held out her glass to him. "Apologies. Pour us another, won't you?"

He took her glass and rose to do her bidding. "I understand you are now a woman of interest. A spinster by choice. An heiress with options. Men seek to gain your favor, hoping you'll appear interested so that they can propose, and you, on the off chance, will bolt and they will gain a small fortune."

"That's very unkind," she told him with remorse only for herself.

He returned and handed her the glass. "But very true."

She downed another sip of brandy. "That now affects Millicent's chances too. Papa hears that men may now think she will do the same as I. Those assertive folks in trade, you know. Such n'er do wells. Which is ridiculous. Who wants to get engaged just for the fun of it?"

"Indeed. Engaged is as good as married." He stared down at her. "But think on it, do. Among the *ton*, land and possessions pass intact with the marriages, controlling the masses at home and shaping the alliances in Parliament and the politics of Britain. To break the rituals and rights of marriage is to break the British social order. My dear, you cannot do that and get away with it. Not for all the money in the world."

"But I have."

"And now you pay for it."

"What am I to do? Allow myself to marry any chap who appeals only to learn later that he drinks or gambles or takes mistresses and leaves me alone at home to…to rot…or breed while he has fun?!"

"Come now. Don't you think you have better instincts than to choose a fellow who will treat you badly?"

"I do! I did. That's why I didn't marry them!"

"I mean, why didn't you follow your instinct *before* you accepted their proposals?"

"I was blind, Harry. In a whirl. Caught up in the euphoria of being courted and danced with and flirted with. It's a crush, you must know."

"I would guess it is. Since I was off to Calcutta, I have no such knowledge. But I do know what it is to find another attractive and to want and to yearn and to be carried along by desire."

"Well! There you have it. Even a man can fall for romance. It's love one wants. So then. Here we are," she announced in triumph, "we've come to an agreement."

"We have?" He cocked a long brown brow at her and took another drink.

"You will not marry for less than love. Neither will I. And between us, we have not love, but a fond childhood friendship. We challenge each other. We make each other work. We do not make each other tingle. So there you are!"

He walked away and poured a third fill into his glass. He frowned, silent as he emptied the decanter. But he did not pick up his glass, only stared at it. "What did you know of those two men whom you accepted?"

"They were...are...fine fellows. A viscount. The other a baron, distinguished, the family descended from a Norman lord. Above my touch, many said, I know they did. Nonetheless both men were good. No major debts. No family scandals. No mistresses hiding in cupboards."

His left eye twitched at that last, but he cleared his throat. "But what did you know of them? Did you race against them? Play chess? Cards? Fence?"

"As you and I did?" She warmed to the memories of their companionship, easy escapades. "No. It was afternoon tea and dances and balls, then a proposal in the moonlight."

"Did you kiss them?"

"Oh, yes."

Jealousy bloomed like an evil flower. He stared at her, nary a move of a hair on his head, until he said, "And?"

She tipped her head to and fro. "Brief."

"Of course. One cannot be caught alone doing that. Was that all?"

She narrowed her eyes. "One pecked. Wet. Like a sick hen."

Both his brows rose as laughter played about his generous mouth. "Tsk-tsk. Bad form. And the other?"

She winced. "Sad."

"As in...?"

"He landed on my nose." She wrinkled her own. "Have you ever had someone kiss your nose?"

He grimaced. "One of my mother's lap dogs."

She closed one eye and shuddered. "Not romantic."

He barked in laughter. "So...no tingles?"

"Oh, you are exasperating, Harry! You are twenty-six years old, fresh from the Continent. You cannot tell me, sir, that you know nothing of attraction or..."

"Tingles."

"Exactly."

He gazed into his full glass and put it down on the sideboard. "I wager that if you had taken matters in to your own hands, things would have been different."

"You mean that I should have kissed them?"

"Why not?"

"Unladylike," she supplied.

"You know how to kiss."

That made her blow air from her startled mouth. "Oh, poor form of you to bring that up!"

He had the very devil dancing in his gaze. "I do, because *you do* know how."

"That was when I was sixteen."

"I bet you're better at it now."

She bristled. "Oh, how could you remind me. Trying to shame me, are you?" She shot to her feet. "I'll go. We will talk tomorrow."

"My dear, do sit down."

She debated. "I have *not* gone around kissing fellows since you left."

"I would have thought you would. You were good at it and enjoyed it."

Her cheeks were on fire. "Stop that."

He chuckled. "I won't tease you any longer, Sara. Please do sit and we will talk on this."

She resumed the chair. "There is not much more to say."

"But there is. You know how to kiss. They did not. On that basis, you concluded—and rightly so—your married life would be…" He waved a hand in the air.

"Boring."

"To say, my dear, the very least."

She snorted. "To say the *very most*, I bet it was Papa's money that made them tingle! Before, during and after the proposal."

"Aside from criticizing your lovely self, darling, you have a poor opinion of men. A man does not ask just any woman to marry him."

"Nor does a woman accept a proposal easily. But I had a need for a…"

He sent her a rueful grin. "Proposal?"

"A tingle."

"I see. Well, then the answer to our dilemma stands before you."

Her gaze ran over him as he flung out his arms in invitation. His insouciant stance meant only one thing. "No."

"Why not?"

"Unnecessary. We are friends, Harry."

"Kiss me and be certain."

She scoffed.

"Call this an experiment. One more man's kisses to add to your list of forgettable moments." He settled his hands on the bare points of his hips.

A wicked gleam in his eyes caused a little tickle to ripple up her spine. Very well. She squared her shoulders.

"Come here."

~

If she thought she could kiss him with impunity, she was wrong. His task was to show her how very wrong.

She'd been too bold to come here half dressed. Too careless to think he didn't care about her or remember what they had meant to each other. Friends, yes.

But in the past few years in letters she'd sent him, she had become more to him. His solace. His lifeline to normality. His connection to a humanity that he often forgot. Slicing open other men, watching the life leak out of them was a savage existence. It reduced one to the barest emotion, not even an eye for an eye. But death for life. How could anyone remain ethical or moral in the bloody business of murdering others?

She was the embodiment of all that was gay and civilized, his past personified with laughter on her lips and defiance in her eyes. He welcomed all she could bring into his embrace.

She rose. Her unbound breasts, larger than when she was a sylph at sixteen, jiggled beneath the silk. Her health, her vitality, her gumption had tempted him to take her in his arms from the moment he'd opened his door. That rapture had been too brief. She came now, wary at his invitation, one careful step at a time.

He could smell her, the traces of her rose *eau de toilette* filling his nostrils with the need to inhale her essence. The anticipation of putting his lips to her skin made him salivate. She was delectably plump, a golden-haired goddess, better than the giggling child with long white blonde tresses. And she thought she could do this easily? This business of getting him to release her from the prospect of marrying him? Refusing him a kiss would be easier, for he'd let her go. But she would never turn away from a dare. She'd kiss him now and perhaps often.

She might not have set a toe over the line of etiquette with those other idiots who had flubbed their chances with her, but he was no callow boy. No child without an idea how to lure. Not like that boy who had kissed her before he sailed away to war. That day, he had not seduced her. He hadn't known how.

Long ago just as tonight, she had come to him in her naiveté as his friend. As she always had. At four years old, a cherub who ambled along beside him to catch fish. At ten, a torment who slipped tadpoles in his breeches when she caught him swimming alone, his clothes abandoned on the bank of the river. At sixteen, a euphoric chit who urged him to kiss her goodbye.

He had. Then never forgot it.

How could he?

She stood before him, within reach, as she had not been for all the years he had pined for her. This moment, this act would be the one that sealed her fate and his. He didn't want to rush her, shock or appall her. Just give her a hot drink of the ambrosia called desire.

He stepped against her, his arms sliding around her waist, one hand up to support her back. He suppressed his shudder. But his erection told her tales he would not utter. That impact of want was hers to learn and his to teach. If indeed she might want him...and feel the tingle.

Against her, he matched his legs to hers, his thigh inserted between her two, bracing her for what he dared to take.

Her lips parted. In flickers of candlelight, her eyes shone brightly into his as she searched for what he'd give.

He brushed his mouth on hers.

She opened, sighed. And lifted her mouth to his for more.

He kissed the corner of her lips, afraid he'd gobble her up and forever chase her away. But she moved with him and found his lips herself. The invitation was one he could not refuse.

He captured her mouth in a ravishing swoop. His arms

crushing her close, he felt the wealth of her breasts and the swell of her belly. All of this and he needed more.

He broke away, mad for breath, and she seized her own at the same time. Again, he had to have her. This time, he teased his tongue along her seam and she opened so easily that he was inside, caressing the warm cavern of her.

She let her head fall back, struggling for air. He leaned over her, the long gleaming column of her throat and the hollow of her breasts his goal. Everywhere, she was soft, succulent, a feast. She clutched him close, her roving hands agile and urgent.

But Christ, this had to end. He could not have her here. Not fast or without benefit of clergy. He might have his father's consent and her sire's, but without hers, they would be nothing.

As he drew up and away and cupped her chin and smiled at her, he knew what he had to do.

"What do you say, my darling? Did you tingle?" That was the silliest question he'd ever asked because he could feel the hard points of her nipples smashed against his chest. If he were rash and crude, he'd draw up her nightrail and press two fingers inside her to confirm that she did more, much more, than tingle.

She met his gaze boldly. "No."

He nodded. She'd always been honest. "I didn't think so."

She stepped backwards and swayed. "We haven't decided what we are going to do about this agreement between your father and mine."

"No." *You haven't? But I have.* "To be decided tomorrow."

31

*S*ara's latest dance partner bowed over her hand. "Delightful. Might I call upon you tomorrow, Miss Fleming?"

"You may, Lord Carrigan." She'd been warned by her father never to refuse a man who wished to appear during afternoon hours. Now with the gossip sheet spreading tales about her, she was shocked any man approached her. "We have quite a few attending, don't we, my dear?" She cast a glance at her young sister who'd been told the same.

Millicent was perfection itself as she acknowledged the man. "We've invited Miss Simmons to play for us."

The prospect of listening to the pianist who was the latest rage in Bath did not put a twinkle in the man's eye. *Ah, he'd heard of the thumping the Simmons woman could deliver to a pianoforte.*

"How wonderful. I look forward to the afternoon."

Any man who enjoyed the abuse the renowned pianist imparted to Hayden or Brahms had to be deaf or dumb.

"Until tomorrow, then." Sara smiled and inclined her

head to politely send him on his way to another dance partner.

"Anyone who endures our events these days," Millie murmured behind her fan, "must be mad with love for one of us."

The two had devised the scheme to invite poor musicians to their afternoon events without their father's knowledge. Since their sire hardly attended tea time and never attended balls such as this one by the illustrious Lord and Lady Gainesville, the sisters had few worries. But such a ruse was the one way to test the waters of men's true affections for Millie, if not also for older, less marriageable Sara.

"You've not had any proposals lately," Millie said with a saucy tease in her sea blue eyes.

"Neither have you, dearest." Sara fanned herself over the worry of it. "A few should come soon."

"There are no men here whom I'd accept." Millie was a cool number, surveying the ocean of this year's dandies and disdaining one and all.

"Take your time. No rush. You'll live with whomever you choose for decades. Enough time to learn every foible he has."

"And he, mine."

"Here comes Lord Wingate, once more."

Millie laughed gaily. "He's a terrible dancer. But I do adore his wit."

"You can teach a man to dance, sweetheart, but you can't improve his humor."

Millie cocked a brow at her. "Good advice. If only I could feel something other than the giggles."

"A tingle, perhaps?" Sara ventured with a vivid memory of the rolling thrill that had rushed through her bloodstream two nights ago.

"A tingle. Yes. But how to get it."

"Kisses."

Millie gave a laugh. "What would I give for one?"

"Take two or three to make certain," Sara confirmed as the witty Lord Wingate bowed before her sister and swept her away to the chalked floor.

"A fine looking couple, wouldn't you say?" Lord Marchant said as he sidled close to her side.

"Good evening, my lord." He had appeared at the last two at-homes she'd attended and here this evening. One of her two jilted grooms, he had conversed with her at length on those previous occasions and caused a few matrons to buzz like bees. His approach to her here tonight would certainly stir the hive. "How are you?"

"Well. Quite well. I like the looks of Wingate and your sister. Wingate, you may know, is my cousin."

"I didn't." She focused on the gentleman before her as a few matrons noted his approach to her and whispered behind their fans.

Marchant hovered close. A fine looking man who was polite and very kind to her, his had been the second proposal she had accepted. "He is very fond of her."

"He does appear to be." Fear stung her that Millie might be reluctant to chose a man, fearing she'd fail at marriage. All because of Sara's inability to decide on a husband.

"He does not dance very gracefully," Marchant said. "I offered to help him. Poor boy."

The 'poor boy' had a baronetcy, a house in London, one in Yorkshire and fourteen thousand a year.

"You know a good dancing instructor?"

"I do." He grinned and an imp emerged. "Myself."

She clapped her hands. "Oh, wonderful, sir. You'd do that for him."

"He is afraid, Sara, that what happened between you and

me may have made such a bad mark against him that no grace on the dance floor would improve his odds."

Carefully, she trod into this territory. "He is his own man, my lord. If he cares for her, he should carry on regardless of my rejection of your proposal."

"He fears, Sara, that she will reject him out of hand because she thinks he courts her only to gain a monetary reward for the effort."

Her heart ached at that. "Terrible for him to feel so constrained. But good of him to carry on and ask her to dance, nonetheless."

"I told him he should. He must. Men do not find a woman they adore so easily. When one does, it is important to pursue the feeling, come what may in the end. Otherwise, one will never know if the person is the right one." He paused and sweetly beheld her. "I do not know why you jilted me, Sara."

She shifted, her frown as deep as her sorrow.

"You did not tell me, Sara. I would like to know. I liked you. Still do. Very much and I—"

"Please, my lord." She looked him in the eye. He was sad and she was guilt-ridden.

"I was 'Reginald' to you. I'd like to be again."

But you took my refusal like a man. And took the compensation my father offered.

She offered him what she could. "I wish we could be friends."

"It was that kiss, wasn't it? Too brief. I should have shown you how I really feel and swept you into my—"

"Oh, Reginald. Please."

"It can be good between us again, Sara. I returned the money your father offered me."

"What?"

"Today. I sent the draft to him. I could not take it. I told

35

my own sire it was not the way I wished to be remembered to you. Or by you. I want us to be as we were, Sara."

She sniffed back her tears and looked up into his very angular, but very dear face. He had been the one who had pecked her on the nose. "That is so good of you, Reginald. I commend you."

"Why not give us another chance, eh? Come dance with me. After all, dancing is a way to a woman's heart. And if Millie can be charmed by it, so can any number of other young women."

That surprised her. "I shouldn't. We shouldn't."

"I disagree. If we do, it will appear that we have become friends."

"You know it won't be only that."

"Neither of us," he went on, "can continue searching for another with impunity, if it appears that we are unreconciled to the unusual end of our relationship."

"Oh, Reginald. If you suffer because of how I treated you, I am sorry. When I ran from the church, I did not intend that you should become…unmarriageable."

He took her hand and squeezed it. "I did not think ill of you then. Nor do I now. Shall we?"

The gossip mongers would have a festival if she were to accept. But for his approval by any lady whom he wished to court—and for his cousin's, she would do it. "For the fun of it. Yes," she said, smiling broadly at him. "We shall."

As they turned for the floor, the tall well-dressed gentleman who approached them halted in his tracks. His hazel eyes meeting hers, then Reginald's, Harry gave her a courteous bow. "Miss Fleming. My lord."

The three exchanged brief pleasantries. Marchant followed with an explanation that they would return after this set.

Sara noted the polite acceptance in Harry's expression as they passed him.

"You dance well together," Harry said after Reginald left her in his care. "Had you much practice when you were betrothed?"

She looked pensive. "No. We should have danced more than we did."

He had to know more. His own suit demanded he have all benefits to his quest. "If he had shown more grace, would you have married him?"

She shook her head. "Grace was not the asset I required. I felt no—"

"Tingles. Yes. I remember."

She fluttered her fan and watched Millie in a circle of Reginald's cousin and two other gentlemen, both London swells of whom he did not approve. He wondered if she knew of their profligate ways.

"How is your mother?" She changed the subject. "I'm certain it was rewarding to see her and be home again."

"It was. My mother is grieving, but coping. She allows herself her time to be quiet and ponder the loss of her oldest child. She sends her greetings and her apologies that she cannot make the journey here. She is not up to the social niceties of engagements."

"She knows then? What your father and mine propose?"

"She does. She is not an advocate of forced marriages, but she tolerates my father's foibles. She loved George." Distaste flashed through him.

Sara pondered his expression and he wished he were less open to her understanding of him. "A mother loves all her children. To lose one in the prime of his life is not the natural way of things. George was always so happy. Delightful company."

"Indeed," he said with a tight expression, ignoring the thousand explanations he wished to add.

Sara paused, her keen gaze searching his. "What's the matter?"

His clothes grew much too tight. They were new, but a finger to the stock at his neck gave him no relief from the constraints that his frivolous, indulgent brother had put upon him.

"You do look very fine in your new tailoring."

"A man home from Spain has a need for one quick with a needle and thread."

"But the fit bothers you."

"No. Other matters cling too tightly to my person."

"Our so-called engagement is a bad fit for me too."

"Not only that."

"What then? We're friends, Harry. You shared much with me in your letters, why not tell me whatever this is?"

He twitched at the stigma cast upon him. "Because it is my family's disgrace."

She was taken aback. "What? I know of no such thing."

"You would not. Perhaps your father does. But I hope not. I do sincerely hope no one does."

She laid a hand upon his arm. "Harry?"

"We should dance."

"Dance? No. You must share this problem."

"Sara, do not concern yourself."

"But I do. What disturbs you, Harry, upsets me."

"Not this."

"A burden shared is one lessened. You wrote that to me when I sent word of my first proposal. Do tell me, Harry."

"Not easily done."

"Disgrace in the Meredith family? Never was one more

upright. But I do wonder. Has your father has fallen into debt? Is that why he needs this arrangement between him and my—"

"Yes."

"But your father is such a prudent man, he never would gamble. Or did he make a poor investment? One of those Far Eastern schemes? A mining venture or—"

"No. Not my father. Never would he risk his money at a table. Nor throw it away on a fantastical scheme. George. George did this to us. To himself."

"He left debts?"

Harry scoffed. "More than!"

Others took note of their discussion. This would be reported in scandal sheets.

Her hand went to his sleeve once more. "Tell me."

He set his jaw and stared down at her. "One does not discuss one's brother's mistresses and a child in the ballroom of one of the premier families of Bath."

She blinked at his revelation. "Indeed not. Let's stroll, shall we, toward the punch bowls?" And at that, she curled her arm around his elbow and headed them toward the far tables near the terrace doors.

CHAPTER 4

$\mathcal{H}$e poured two cups of the ratafia punch. He hated this admission of the family disaster, unused as he was to such dishonor. "I should not have told you," he said, handing her the cup.

"It is not your shame."

"We have a reputation to uphold. The house of Meredith does not commit such acts."

"I dare say we all have peccadilloes we wish to forget."

He appreciated her sympathy and her touch of humor. "Not you."

"Others think so."

"You did nothing to merit ridicule, only decided not to marry."

"The implication is that I have something to hide. A secret worth keeping from a husband."

He took a swig of the punch. "Gad. Terrible stuff."

She made a face. "I'd prefer a good whisky."

"Let's see if we can find something worthy of us, shall we?"

She cast a glance back at her sister. "A few minutes, yes."

"Her friend there will take care of her."

He watched her catch Millicent's eye and nod to her. The girl returned a smile to Sara.

They took the length of the ballroom into the hall. A few couples strolled past them. Nothing scandalous could be construed from their proximity. When they stopped at the end of the hall and the open doors to the orangery, no one was about.

"I do not wish to speak of the reasons why my father made this bargain with yours. It is irrelevant to what you and I face together."

"Hardly irrelevant, Harry. Not if your father gains money from the pact!"

"I doubt it has exchanged banks yet."

She drew back. "There is time? What a comfort."

"Don't count on it. I've no idea what I can do, but I must find something to stop this."

She strode into the orangery, frustrated at the challenges he and she faced. The fragrance of orange and lemon trees refreshed her spirit, if only for a moment. The maze of potted ferns and roses had her weaving toward the tall Palladian windows that overlooked a garden swathed in the velvet black of night and twinkling stars. Two window-paned doors stood open. She went to stand near an open portal and let the evening breezes flow about her. The chill of her predicament had her rubbing her bare arms. She should have continued to dance all night, but why when Harry was much better company and needed her.

He removed his evening coat and draped it over her shoulders. "You must not worry. I will not marry you under these circumstances."

His hands on her shoulders brought comfort. His familiar essence of sandalwood and citrus rose to fill her with more solace.

"I told my mother. She understands."

"I'm grateful," she said at last.

"But she's not happy." He turned her to him. "You're not. Nor am I."

"The truth is I must marry someone and soon. Millie's future depends on it."

"I agree." He wrapped her close in his embrace, a hand to her bare shoulders, another to her nape. His tenderness purled through her like the slow soft babble of a stream. "Listen to me, Sara. I have a plan. It won't be one either of our fathers likes but it might work."

She pulled away. Peering into his magnificent eyes clouded her judgement. His green-brown orbs reflected a sadness in the faint lights that matched her own. "Tell me."

"We announce that we intend to marry others."

"But the story in the *Gazette*—?"

"Hang them at the *Gazette*."

"We'll send them new stories. Marvelous. I like your thinking, Harry. Marry another. Ba! Precisely *who* did you have in mind?"

He gave her a look that said he had the right answer. "A man who makes you tingle."

"Of whom there is no one." *Which is a lie.*

"For each woman, there is a man. A perfect match."

"I've not found him in four years. Why now?"

"You will lure him."

By some folly, to be sure. "How?"

A wicked gleam lit those iridescent eyes. "With kisses."

"You expect me to kiss men?"

He shrugged a shoulder. "How else will you discover the right fellow?"

"How else will I go down as a scarlet woman? I've climbed enough fences barring me because I am of the dreaded merchant class. Papa's money might continue to buy

42

me entry, but if I degrade myself further, no one will touch me!"

He tipped up his chin. "You will be discreet. I will help."

"You'll bar doors?"

"And divert traffic."

She scowled at him. "You've been away much too long, sir. You think me so brave. I am different from that child who tagged along behind you and tucked frogs in your pants."

He scoffed. "Remind me. Who came to me night before last in her nightrail?"

"Dressing gown."

He waved that away. "Exactly my point."

Exasperated, she huffed. "The fault, dear Harry, is not in our stars, but in myself."

"I agree."

Oh, he infuriated her! "I do not know how to kiss."

"And so you will learn."

Only one way. She could barely say it. "By doing."

"Indeed." He winked. "With me."

That way lay disaster and hopeless ruin. She'd given up wanting him so long ago. Or thought she had. She threw up her hands. "Absurd."

"Is it?" He took a step toward her, so near she inhaled his scent, imbibed his familiar allure that she could not allow to thrill her. "You said my kiss left you with no...what is the word?"

"You know perfectly well the word."

"Tickle?"

If only. "Tingle."

"Well then, my darling." With one hand he caught her wrist while he swept his other hand around her waist. "Let's see if this fits the bill."

43

"No, stop!" *Wonderful.* Now she sounded like the village crier.

"There, there. Don't be shy. An experiment, eh?" He lifted her hand toward his mouth. "Or shall we call it..." he murmured, as he put her index finger, fully gloved, against the neat cleft in his chin, "...a demonstration? Visible to the naked eye."

He smiled. Or was that the show of teeth of a predator? A creature who...gloated?

He caught the point of her glove between his long white incisors. The act of a male bent on taking a bite of her, he tugged. The fabric slid along her finger, silk on silk, a glissade of shivering delight. Her glove glided from her elbow in a silent skim of her nerves. She shivered. He halted. Glanced up at her, those long dark lashes of his rising to reveal the facets of a Harry she'd never known. A ravenous devil appeared there, one who pulled at another fingertip, starving for more of her until her hand was bare. Nipping her third finger and the next, he sent tremors up her spine. Her mouth fell open as he took her smallest finger, fabric and all, and bathed the whole of it in his hot moist mouth. His tongue served as succor—and as torture.

She panted as if she'd run a mile. Her gaze glued to his voracious teeth, she dare not look away or lose a second. What he gave, she took. If it was instruction, it was also a revelation. Though she knew not how to interpret his lips to her fingers as lips to lips, she reveled in whatever he'd choose next.

With a yank of his teeth, he pulled and her glove slid slowly down her arm and fell to the floor. She was bare to the night air, chilled and burning, as he caught her fingers and pressed them to his open mouth. He groaned and crushed her torso fully against him. His possession, from her breasts to her hips, left her pulsing.

He put her palm to his lips and licked the hollow of her hand. She moaned at his luscious homage and her knees gave way. As he caught her up, he bit the heal of her hand. She yelped. He gave a grunt, nigh unto laughter or triumph, she knew not which, then wrapped her arm around his waist. As he sweetly backed her to the wall, his hair fell loose over his brow and he focused on her lips.

Then he took them.

This kiss was fierce. A capture of her flesh. A press of firm lips, the intrusion of his tongue, a slide, a caress. A moan welled up in her throat. She needed him, lips, arms, legs. He yanked away and breathed her name. A raw pant from each met the other and they were once again, moving, tasting, sharing.

His tongue probed her mouth, sweeping the caverns and taking more of her precious breath. His hands molded her against him, her breasts flat and aching against his chest. He lifted her leg, moved it to one side and stepped in.

She gasped and nestled into his rigid erection. This, beyond her wildest imaginings, surpassed the meager sensation of a tingle.

He moved to have her again. He was not done. And she was so glad.

His next kiss was slow. A benediction, followed by the bestowal of a thousand tiny kisses. His mouth nibbled hers, seizing the fullness of her lower lip, then withdrawing. A tide upon her flesh. An erosion of all thought.

With a start, he drew back. "Look at me."

She had no will to do other.

"That is one way to kiss."

She clung to the wall. No other means held her up except his thrall.

He smiled, but the sentiment was brief. Then he touched the tip of her nose. "We'll do this again."

She stared at him, the raw power of her enchantment driving her to torment him and herself. She wanted tonight, all night. But must not. *Must not.* "Tomorrow."

"At ten." He gave a nod and shot his cuffs. "My house. Papa has gone home. I'll send the servants out."

Assured, wasn't he? She rallied. "You won't be surprised if I don't come."

"You need more instructions."

Need. Want. What did it matter? "I cannot do this again."

"Afraid?"

"I wanted a tingle."

"No demonstrations then. Only descriptions."

She shivered. What could he say with words that might equal the thrill of this that they'd shared? "That would be preferable."

"Fine. Bring your purse."

"Why?"

If he'd acted like a wild creature before, he was a demon now. "I have to be paid for my services in some way, don't I?"

She laughed freely. "You are no mercenary."

"I've been away with hundreds of men who have few other ways to spend their time. I'm good at gambling."

That seized her breath. "Why?"

"Just being sporting. And you always liked a good bet."

She frowned. "On this?"

"If you won't come any other way, yes."

If this was how he wanted to play, who was she to fight it? "Very well. What is the game?"

"Chess."

"Ha! You are a terrible player, Harry. I will win."

"Try it then. You've nothing to lose, right?"

"Chess, it is. For what prize?"

He sauntered near, and brushed his thumb around her throbbing lips. "If I win? All the kisses I can demonstrate."

That should have sent her to her knees in thanksgiving. But she'd been blessed with stubbornness and strong legs. "If I win…"

Sanguine, he raised his brows in challenge. "What will you want?"

"One night together."

Shock drained the blood from his features. "Why?"

"Because…" *After I leave your bed, I'll never want another's.* "Because I doubt any man I'd want will ever care for me. Only my father's money."

CHAPTER 5

*P*laying against himself. He knew he was.

Moving his black pawn forward to counter the advance of the white knight, Harry flinched that he felt more the pawn than a knight in this game he had so rashly proposed.

He glanced at the clock on the mantle. Ten minutes after ten. He'd lost all already. She would not come.

Why would she?

He offered her what she wanted. One of her cursed tingles. Then got carried away.

He blew a gust of air from his lips and darted from his chair to glance out the window toward the Green. A light rain had fallen since early morning and turned the grass greener. Not so was his life.

"Not unless I can show her that what I want is not her lust. But a state much more grand."

Yet now, mutton-head that he was, how to prove it?

He stared back at his board. His black knight could leap over to threaten his white pawn. But then the white bishop would have an advantage. The bishop...

Exactly! The bishop.

Why did that irritate him?

Footsteps along the hall had his head coming up.

She appeared, a wraith in geranium pink with a worn shawl of pale white muslin thrown over her head.

He beamed at her in welcome. He might not know what to do with her today—kisses not withstanding—but he could never turn her away. Hand out, he went to her and drew her inside the salon.

"Did you worry I would refuse to come?" She had to tease him, didn't she, to cover her irritation that he had the upper hand. Or rather, the better idea.

"I did," he admitted. "You intended it, I'm sure."

"All's fair." She wiggled her brows, then slid the damp shawl from her hair. Her coif was no more than a loose swirl, a heavy knot threatening to fail. Would that he could take the whole thing down and...

He cleared his throat. "Come sit. See what I've done so far."

As she swept into the old royal blue velvet chair, she wrinkled her nose and surveyed the damage. "You began without me. Tsk-tsk. Did you wish to try my mettle at improving what damage you've wrought?"

"I hoped to get the advantage." He flipped up the tails of his frock coat and sat opposite her. *My god.* She was more beautiful in the plain cotton than in the silks and satins required of the evenings. Even the simple gather of her hair, informal and easy, had him longing to bury his nose in the wealth.

"You have made a muck of it, sir." She rubbed her fingers together and made a tempting moue of those plump pink lips. She caught his gaze and laughed. "I shall challenge your knight."

At her move, he calculated that he'd be conquered in

three or four more. Figuring out how to save himself from being a cad and taking her to bed for a night, he focused on studying the board as if at leisure. "Would you like coffee? Tea?" He indicated the old Italian credence. "I had my butler bring up a few sandwiches before he left."

She sat back, looking about the room and twiddling her thumbs. "What did you do with your servants? Tuck them up in the attic?"

"Locked them in the wine cellar."

She burst into laughter. "Good one. Although I would like to have been there."

He raised his eyes to meet hers. "No, you would not."

"We'd have your choice wines to complement our game."

"We need no alcoholic beverages today."

She rapped her fingers on the table. "I'd welcome spirits."

"What you wager, my dear, needs no embellishments."

"Said he who began this entire charade."

"Taunting me to distract me?"

She feigned innocence with wide eyes and a hand to her delightful bosom. Which, he hated to note that today was covered up to her throat. "Heavens, no."

He mashed his lips together and directed his mind to focus on the board, the game, the odds. He picked up his knight to get him away from her and plunked it down with a flourish. "There!"

"Ha! You don't need a distraction, dear man, to make a bad move." She tapped her finger against her lips. Such a poor thing to do to such a delectable bit. But with an 'ah-ha!', she picked up one of her pawns and made a mess of his strategy to protect his knight.

Frustrated with his master plan, all of them, he worried about her. "You mustn't give up hope."

"That I'll win here?" Her jade eyes did a little dance. "Never a chance."

"I mean," he said and caught her hand, "that no man would want you."

"If you take me to bed, I won't worry about that any longer. I will become a spinster. Crabby Aunt Sara to Millie's brood."

"What's money for if it can't bring you what you most desire?"

She tipped her head. "Well, there was a day when I'd say that myself. Now," she said with a flourish and pointed to the board, "there is this."

"You can't give up."

She fell back. "Are you reneging on our bet?"

"Never."

"Then why aren't you kissing me?"

"Because," he said and lifted his bishop, "we are playing."

She shot to her feet. "Indeed we are." Then she pushed the table to one side, and to his astonishment, sat in his lap.

At once he sported a dry mouth and a very hard cock. Grabbing her arms, he meant to push her away but instinct demanded something else entirely. And he drew her near.

She smiled, the witch, then brushed her mouth over his. "I liked your lessons yesterday. I am in need of more."

"I should send you home."

She moved infinitely closer. "You forfeit then?"

"You're not playing," he rejoined.

"Not any more, no, I'm not." She slid her hands up his chest and circled her long warm fingers around his throat. With tiny murmurs to his ear and his temple, she filled his mind with hopes of her complete surrender. But as her fingers mussed his hair, he became all hers. "Yesterday you taught me to tease a man."

"You do know now how to remove his gloves with your teeth."

She cupped his jaw, chuckled and swooped in for a full

taste of his mouth. "Hmm. You had coffee before I came. It tastes divine. I'd like to have coffee afterward."

She spread kisses to one side of his mouth and then to the other. He could not keep up with her, even if his erection knew exactly where he should lead her. "After...? After what?"

"After I come."

He wanted to rise up, show her the man he should be, but she traced the tip of her tongue along the seam of his lips. "Where...where did you learn such language?"

"Does it matter?" She dipped to the hollow of his throat and licked him.

"*Christ.* No." He tipped up her chin and took her mouth the way he'd imagined when he sat by a campfire, daydreaming with a thousand other men of lovers far away. He moved with her now, caught her under her legs and rose. He'd never walked with such a stone hard cock, but somehow he got them to the settee. There, he sat down and pulled her back between his legs. She'd feel the truth he sought to shield from her, but at least this way he'd keep her a virgin.

"You want me," she whispered in triumph and curled around to claim his mouth. An inch more and her elbow would stick him in the groin and destroy his manhood.

He maneuvered to one side. She followed, sweet torment that she was. "I shouldn't."

With a murmur, she agreed and between kisses, laughed. "But we can forget the game."

"Wanting you is no sport."

"Give in, then, Harry."

Make love to her? "I'd be less than honorable."

She put her hand over his flies, her expression devoid of all humor. "I don't want your honor, Harry."

As if she'd put ice to his skin, loss of honor cooled his

blood. His hand atop hers, he stilled her pursuit. "I do want yours."

He pushed her beneath him and one leg to the floor, he pulled her to her feet. "Time to go."

The look on her face told him he'd gutted her. Well, now there were two ravaged by this turn of events.

"You must leave." He smoothed the wrinkled line of her gown at her chest. How he'd hoped to convince her to marry him without such scenes as this. How to show her he loved her and dare to elicit a declaration of love from her drifted away, just like the abrupt thunder and lightning outside. "We will discover another way to end this charade."

She stiffened. "We must think fast. Papa says he has engaged the vicar and invited breakfast guests."

"Has he?" He put his waistcoat and his breeches to rights. "The date?"

"He didn't say." She frowned. "I should have asked."

"As should I." He swept both hands through his hair. "I have an inkling of something. Truly, whatever it is, there's more to this than the money they exchanged."

"Aside from pride and arrogance? Oh, yes. But you are right. If we are to marry, where is the proof?"

Befuddled and angry, he strode to the window. Those below scurried about in the sudden deluge. "Who sent that information to the news sheet?"

He heard her soft tread upon the carpet. Whirling on her, he put up a hand. "Your appearance here would add a firestorm. Think about the *Gazette*..."

She halted in her tracks. "We must learn who sent that news to them. They had to know a few facts. Our butler? Impossible. A housemaid? She'd be sacked. I know of no one. But I could be wrong. And here? Who here would risk dismissal?"

"Heaven knows." He strode toward her and took her

chilled hands in his. "You're shaking. Let me work on this. Don't worry. Oh, Sara." He took her in his arms and she came without objection.

Nestling there, she rubbed her cheek to his chest. "I was hopeful of defeating you today. Chess, be damned."

He barked in laughter but held her tightly. His lips found the shell of her ear and he kissed her there. "I know. I enjoyed it all, my dear. But we have work to do."

She pulled away, sniffing back what might have been the start of tears. "I have servants to interrogate."

He swiped a thumb over the appealing lips he had savored for far too brief a time. "As do I."

She donned a sprightly air. "And men to kiss."

"Don't," he couldn't stop himself from saying.

She danced backward out of his embrace. "Tonight, the Kirkhams give a musicale. Do you go?"

He shouldn't. In mourning, he should remain home, but he had to be wherever she was. Tonight. Always. "If you do."

"Good." She nodded, her expression filling with the same sweet euphoria she'd exuded when he'd held her beneath him. "Then there will be one man in attendance I plan to kiss."

"At your peril."

She threw him a wink and twiddled her fingers at him in farewell. "And yours, sir."

CHAPTER 6

*T*he Kirkhams rented a house in the Circus. The house was tidy, small, and had the pianist been slightly better, the salon would have suited the melody much better.

Sara and Millie had parted, her sister to a friend and Sara took up a conversation with Lord Marchant. Across the room, Harry held up the wall, his cane assisting him. But she saw what he did. He supervised her with Marchant. So be it. Harry and she had kissed, extensively, and he had an investment in her as much as she did in him.

She decided to wager on how large that investment might be.

And so as the evening wound to a close after the pianist ended her assault on the poor pianoforte, the twenty-odd guests went to the larger salon with a convenient set of doors to a small garden.

"I'm very pleased that you have decided we can be friends, my lord." They stood at the open doors, in full view of others. He'd just delivered a glass of some tasteless white wine and she pretended to like it.

"I like you, Sara. The sum your father gave to me after you decided not to marry me, always felt odd. Money I had taken that should not belong to me. I am grateful he accepted it back."

"He told me today, he values that you returned it. But he meant it in good will."

"I like to think that what I did by returning it puts me in your good graces."

A footman passed with a tray and she put her glass aside. So did Marchant.

"You were always in my good graces, sir."

"Was I?" He stepped toward her.

Blocking her view of those in the salon, she smiled. But grew wary. "I understand you entertained Lord Carrigan at tea today."

"He did attend, yes."

A hint of jealousy flashed across Marchant's brow. "Might I stand a chance with you again? I know there is this talk of the Raven—"

"Oh, you read that bit in the *Gazette* and I do hope you will ignore it. Ravensford and I were childhood friends. I am happy to see him home, of course, but there is no agreement there."

"The tragedy is it mentions money."

"Another payment," she said with derision. "Money seems to follow me around. Too much I think."

He lifted his hand to her chin. "You are too lovely to have such stories connected to you."

"Thank you," she said as his thumb caressed her cheek.

"Sara, I'd like to call on you. Alone."

"My lord, I am not ready to receive you like that."

"If I kissed you as you should be kissed, perhaps you'd welcome me more readily?"

"Oh, I…"

To one corner of her eye appeared the tall, dark-eyed Harry Wallace. Leaning upon his cane, he murmured a sound of apology for intruding, then turned on his heel and left.

Marchant sagged as if the wind had been wrung out of him. "He is everywhere. Shall we go in?"

"We will," she said as she gave him a blithe smile that was more relief than apology.

It was to Harry, she owed one. She thought she could kiss any man for fun, for an education.

She couldn't even summon the desire to kiss a man who had been kind to her, and who at one time, she would have married.

She had to find a way to end this tangle her father and the duke had created. She wanted Harry, only Harry, as her own. Or no other man as her husband.

But only if he loved her.

No other way.

CHAPTER 7

"*Y*ou look terrible." Millie was aghast, a hand out to Sara as she climbed into their carriage.

The ride to church was brief, but a drizzle dampened any idea of walking to town for the morning service. She had no energy for it and was glad for the seclusion of the closed conveyance. Perhaps few would notice her eyes were puffy from crying. "I didn't sleep well."

"You've done your best in this muddle," Millie offered with a poor imitation of a smile. "You are not to blame for what's happened."

Sara fussed with the pillows as she settled into the squabs beside her sister. "Oh, aside from that horrible piece in the *Gazette*, but for all that has followed? I acted brashly. Even last night, with Marchant. Of course, I succeeded. All too well. And Harry? He thinks me flighty and irresponsible. Worse, assuredly. No wonder he doesn't lo... Oh, no matter. I must get a word alone with him this morning."

Her sister licked her lips and winced. "I need a word with you."

Sara let out an exasperated breath. Papa was at the door

talking to their butler, collecting his walking stick, ready to leave and join them for church. "About what?"

"I've been meaning to tell you—"

Sara put her hand over her sister's. "Stop fidgeting. It can't be that bad. Or can it?"

"Terrible."

"What? Ohh! I know. You have a proposal? Is he not a proper fellow? Who—?"

"No, Sara. Not a proposal. The *Gazette*. I wrote that bit. I gave it to them."

Sara's mouth fell open. She could not believe this of Millie. "What?"

"I did." Her sister wiped a fat tear from her cheek.

"Why? Why would you do that?"

"I overheard Papa talking with the duke last week in Papa's study. I knew Harry was coming home and that you and he had loved each other before he left for India."

"But, Millie, to make me a subject of the *ton*?"

"Horrid, it was. Yet I knew no other way. I wanted you to act fearlessly, against Papa's plan. And to be quick about it with Harry. But then there is another matter. Worse. Urgent, too. You see, there are those two women who compete in this wedding wager. They had you on their list to match you with men. I couldn't bear that they'd trick you and lock you to a marriage without love or respect."

She valued her sister's concern and in time, would probably praise her for her action, but she could not fathom the deviousness of a few meddling women to carelessly match-make. "How unscrupulous are these two women?"

"I'm not certain. But I've heard rumors that they bet between them to win a few tiaras. I knew you didn't know about them, Sara. I didn't want you to. You'd call on them and scold them to high heavens. And then what?"

Outrage filled her. "I'd have the most wonderful time doing it."

Millie nodded. "I know! But you'd be banned!"

Her father headed down the front steps toward their coach.

"Did Papa know about this wedding wager?"

"Not at first. The duke told him of it that day they agreed to their plan. The duke said it was a good thing they both arranged this because he was sure Harry would marry you in a heartbeat."

"They were wrong."

Their footman swung open the carriage door for their father.

Millie squeezed her hand and leaned close. "But you love him."

I do. Enough to never marry him without his love in return.

Containing her confusion, Sara entered the abbey and walked with her father and sister to their pew on the left. Nodding in silent greeting to this one and that, they made their way to their usual seats, third from the front. They had only five minutes before the service was to begin and she expected that the duke and Harry would not attend today.

But at the last minute, both men appeared and took the front row. As Harry passed, he inclined his head in greeting to her father and sister. Sara, in a rare case of shyness, did not meet his gaze. What she would say to him would be an apology that would close their relationship forevermore. Money or fathers' bargains or a sister who intervened could not save them from the end.

She listened to nothing. Not the archdeacon's sermon or

the readings. Not the choir or the organist. The hour could not end soon enough, and yet an eternity passed until they stood and began to file down the aisle.

But her father dallied. The Duke of Meredith had waited until he exited their pew and the two of them, long-time friends, chatted as if they hadn't seen each other in years. If it was a show of how they welcomed each other to the fold of their respective families, Sara could only marvel.

At once, Harry was beside her, his hand to her elbow. "We must talk."

She stared at him. "I did not kiss him. It may have appeared that way, but no."

"Oh, my darling."

How could he call her that and make her heart ache so?

Yet he seemed to bubble with joy. All she wanted from him was forgiveness. Nor could she hope for anything more. "I thought on it, Sara. I hoped not."

"I could not."

"How wise of you." He raised his hand appearing as if he'd caress her cheek.

She took his hand, let any see who might construe such familiarity as more than friendship. "Oh, Harry. This whole business is such a mess. Millie is the one who gave the *Gazette* the story."

"Millie? Really! I will have to thank her."

"Thank her? What?" She tried to keep her voice low as more and more parishioners lifted their brows and muttered as they found their conversation intriguing. "No! It's bad enough that our fathers sought to bind us, thinking they did the right thing."

"I know. But they did not do it all." He chuckled.

Was he so relieved he was daft? "Now you talk in riddles."

The party descended toward the narthex and he wound

her arm more securely in his. "Caught in their own net, Sara. They did not do as they should have."

"I don't understand."

"Did you not hear, my darling?"

That endearment again? He had to stop! "Hear what?"

"No banns."

She straightened. Her mind awhirl. She hadn't paid attention. "They called no banns today?"

"None."

She stopped and others muttered as they wove around Harry and her. "So then your father and mine...forgot?" She could swoon in happiness. "You and I are not bound to each other."

He hugged her arm to his solid chest. "Only by that blasted...forgive me, by the money."

And he was grinning. Grinning!

"That's good." *But was it?* Now there was only the money that bound their fathers to a paper. But what of her feelings? *Her love for Harry?*

They emerged into the sunlight. The clouds had parted. Sunlight filled the rain-washed square. The air was fresh. A breeze rippled through the crowd. But she was chilled. Lost. She'd never marry Harry now.

Now with all that money going to his father. She would not be the bought and paid for wife. She would be a cherished bride or no one's. She'd run.

"My father tells me," Harry said as he bent close upon the steps, "the money arrives tomorrow in our accounts. But I promise you, I will return it. Every penny. If I cannot get our banker to return it without my father's approval, I will repay it on my own. Earn it. With profits from sound management. I know not how many years, Sara, but I will not have it said we took money from your father."

He had saved her reputation. Respected her integrity. "Now," she said with utter despair, "we can marry as we like."

He laughed up at the sky and the sun. "Yes, indeed."

She broke from him. A swift step, then a stride, then a scramble through the crowd.

"Wait! Sara!" She could hear him calling, clicking his walking stick against the cobbles, rushing after her.

"I can't keep up. Sara!"

But she could not stop.

Headed toward the shops and the thoroughfare to home, she pushed through crowds. Throngs. Hundreds. *Drat! Where had they come from?*

"Don't go! Wait!" He caught her and hauled her to the edge of the walk as a carriage and a sedan chair passed. "What's the matter? Don't you see? They did not call for the banns, so they have not finalized the marriage. They left one avenue open."

Tears threatened to destroy her public reputation. "To go on our merry way. Of course, I see it. Do take your hands off me, Harry. I wish to walk home alone."

"No, you don't. Not alone. Not any more. I am here. Will stay here, too. So are you going to tell me now how you love me?"

Glaring at him, she tugged at his hold. "You run a fever, Harry."

"For you, I do, yes."

"Stop this."

"I care for you, Sara. In fact, I—"

"Care?" She did screech like an owl, didn't she? "How could you *care* for me?"

"I do care for *you*! I always have."

"Thank you very much. Kind of you, sir. Now if you don't mind—"

"I do mind. I do! I care. I care so much that I love you. I

63

have loved you all my life. All of it! When I was six and ten and fourteen and twenty and all the years in between. I've loved you by a river and in a stable and over a chessboard, in Bath and in Calcutta and Vittoria and here again. Anywhere I've been, I have taken my love for you with me. Anywhere I go, I wish to take you with me from now on. Oh, do you not see? I love you, Sara Fleming." Then he dropped to his knees.

In the walkway upon the cobbles in front of the bakery and the haberdashers', he gazed up at her with hope and those incredible words on his lips. "I love you and I ask you to marry me."

Her ears did work well. But her mind had a hard time listening. "You are attracting a crowd, Harry."

"As long as I attract you, I'm happy."

"Are you?" She should giggle, like a girl. But then, she liked the idea. "I'm happy with you at the moment. And to be honest, I rather like you myself."

"Tease." He gave a laugh and pulled at her hand. "Tell me, might you love me?"

She considered the sea of inquiring faces before her, then examined the clear blue sky and the birds flying high. He peered up at her, his hazel eyes dark with worry. He was anxious, her handsome Harry. "There is no 'might' about it."

He fought with a smile. "So you'll marry me?"

She tipped her head to one side. "We have to call the banns."

He shot to his feet and wrapped his arms around her, right there in the main thoroughfare of Bath. "To bloody hell with banns, my love. I'll get a special license."

What a good man. She circled her arms around his shoulders and brushed her lips on his. "I'm free Friday."

And so on that Sunday in August before approximately a hundred citizens of the city of Bath, the new Earl of Ravensford kissed the eldest daughter of the whisky king, Dashiell Fleming.

"Friday," the groom-to-be confirmed. "In your father's parlor. At ten o'clock."

She chuckled. "I will be there."

And she was.

THE END

LORD STANTON'S SHOCKING SEASIDE HONEYMOON

LORD STANTON'S SHOCKING SEASIDE HONEYMOON

First published with the Bluestocking Belles in their connected anthology, **Storm & Shelter**, *this story is dear to my heart. It has also won many awards for its endearing characters. Enjoy!*

She is so wrong for him.

Miss Josephine Meadows is so young. In love with life. His accountant in his work for Whitehall. Her father's heir to his trading company—and his espionage network.

Lord Stanton cannot resist marrying her. But to ensure Wellington defeats Napoleon, they must save one of Josephine's agents.

Far from home, amidst a horrific storm, Stanton discovers that his new bride loves him dearly.

Can he truly be so right for her?
And she for him?

DEDICATION

So often the work of writing historical fiction depends on the help of colleagues who are experts in finite facts. Here author Elizabeth Essex aided me with her invaluable understanding of nautical issues.
Thank you, Elizabeth

CHAPTER 1

Tuesday, March 28, 1815
Stanton House
Grosvenor Square, London

*a*s Russell Arthur Fenwick Downey, the sixth earl of Stanton, glanced among those seated at his dining room table the night before his second wedding, he understood the myriad permutations of the saying, to marry in haste and repent at leisure.

He inhaled, stealing himself to suffer the rudeness of his mother and younger brother. He could name each anew, dubbing Mama Stuffy and his brother, Clifford, Dandy. Opposite them in every way sat his fiancée, whom for her kindness in spite of them, he would name Merciful. And since he was to be the most fortunate man in the Realm after he wed her tomorrow morning in her father's house, he would call her Beloved—and thankfully, joyfully, at-long-last His.

For after tomorrow at nine o'clock, he would know the rewards of having waited until long after she'd come of age, this sprightly woman of twenty-four who laughed so easily and who had reminded him just yesterday afternoon that she was a perfect match for him.

"A trader's daughter?" Her large grass green eyes had twinkled at him in mirth. "I know maths better than I can recite your ancestry, dear sir. Plus," she said, marveling as she held up her wooden darning egg and worn sock upon it, "I am expert at mending clothes."

He'd assured her that her skills at such were most welcome in his house, where her good cheer and boundless energy for life had mended his heart and his belief in the rightness of the human spirit. God knew, he had proof—too much—of the other.

"Where do you go for your wedding trip?" His mother finished her *blanc mange* and Russ could count the minutes until this blasted meal was done.

Josephine's fork paused at the question.

"We've postponed any trip, Mama."

The Countess of Stanton stared first at her soon to be daughter-in-law, then at him. Did she suppress the haughty smile that tugged at her lips? "Why would you do that?"

His left eye twitched. The old injury caught him in times of stress. This certainly was one as he could take bets at White's that she saw how he adored his future wife but would not bed her until she appeared eager for such a union. But he could not let his mother intimate it, lest he harry her to the street and her carriage, not to return until he righted the problem.

"Napoleon, my lady." Josephine reminded his mother of the scourge of their days and nights. "We are beset with grave matters now that he's returned to France."

"Stanton's challenge I do understand, Miss Meadows." His mother trained her dour brown eyes on his. Like a crown, she wore her pride in his position as adviser to the Secretary at War. Though she suspected, he doubted she knew his full role as advisor to the Army Commissariat for supply of Wellington's Army in the Low Countries. But she was being purposely obtuse on this point of the wedding trip, solely to embarrass his future wife and snidely to ridicule her father. "Surely, Stanton, for your wedding, you might take a few days to become better acquainted?"

Ah, and there is the rub. From my mother, no less, who knows I met my fiancée six years ago but who wants to drive a wedge between us. He massaged his left temple. "Josephine and I have agreed that we will retire to the country house in Bury St. Edmonds after we have defeated the man."

His brother Clifford snorted. "That may take years."

"I doubt it," Josephine replied with such speed and assurance that both his relatives glared at her. Women, they believed, particularly daughters of merchants, were not worthy to claim such opinions. But because of her commanding position in her father's company, Josephine was. Neither was she cowed by their shock. Instead, she took a sip of her own muscat and smiled at them. "Napoleon has little with which to carry on the fight now. Fewer soldiers who are willing to die for him. Worse, he has little money to fund them."

"You've read, Mama, I'm certain, that Louis and his court have fled Paris. And wise of him, he had presence of mind to take the French treasury with him." The Army Commissariat's courier who arrived from Ostend yesterday, expected Louis to reach there today or tomorrow, trailing an immense baggage train behind him. Gold bullion, all hoped, would be among the contents.

"I would bet they took the crown jewels, too," Josephine added on a chuckle. "Worth fourteen million francs. Can you imagine?"

His mother tutted. "You have this from your father, Miss Meadows?"

"No, Ma'am. I do not." Josephine's sharp gaze glanced off Russ's.

That fact she'd had from her own courier, one of the last to sail from besieged Calais. She'd shared the news with Russ earlier today when they'd met in her father's offices in Dawson Street. Her father's deteriorating health had turned Josephine into the head of Meadows Trading Company. Her father's suggestion before Christmas that Russ ask for Josephine's hand was occasioned by her father's worries over her future and his deteriorating health. Russ had taken the man's advice not only because Meadows had indicated that his daughter would welcome the union, but also because Russ had fallen in love with her from the first day he'd met her.

"I do hope you are not delaying any travel because you are ill."

"No," was his clipped reply.

His mother's concern was a dry declaration that posed a question beneath. Russ knew what it was because his mother had demanded an answer to this last week. Then, she'd not been so subtle.

"Why did you acquire a special license to marry her?" His mother had asked him after he'd appeared in her drawing room and announced his impending nuptials. "The wedding was set for June."

"Her father fears his imminent demise. He wishes to see his girl married."

"To you? Of course, he would! A marquess for his lowly *cit*."

Biting his tongue, he readied to take his leave. "Excuse me, Mama. I have urgent business."

She shook with anger. "No other urgent reason for this date?"

He fought to contain his ire. "None."

She'd sniffed. "I don't suppose you'd tell me anyway if she were *enciente.*"

"Good day, Mama." He was fed to the gills with her opposition to his marriage. "Come to meet her next Tuesday evening for dinner. I've invited Clifford up from Brighton. Attend only if you wish to be civil."

Without waiting for her reply, he'd spun for the foyer, her butler, his hat and walking stick.

That she was here tonight and rude was testament to her tenacity to ruin this union.

Yet he would never let that happen.

"Shall we adjourn to the drawing room?" He shot to his feet. The others followed. "We must have an early start tomorrow."

CHAPTER 2

*J*osephine stood when Stanton returned to the drawing room after showing his mother and brother to the door. In hopes to appear nonchalant, she gave him a cheery smile. But the tensions at dinner aroused such fear in her. "I'm not good at hiding my feelings. I hope I did not offend your mother."

"She was the one who offended you." He took her cold hands in his warm ones, the corners of his appealing mouth turned up in consolation. "I know how intimidating my mother can be. Allow me to apologize for any discomfort."

"Oh, Stanton. She does not want to like me. I am so unacceptable." *I am her nightmare.* "She wished for you a young woman of more stature than I."

His long fingers crushed her fidgeting ones. "She has little acquaintance with marriage for the sake of affection."

So she would not understand that I marry for the sake of love. "She does not know how to excuse me to her friends."

"Once they see how kind and quick you are, they will love you."

As you do? The question, ever on her mind for more than a

year, burned through her. When he'd proposed Christmas day, he'd not declared his affections as more than that. Admiration for her fealty to her father. Respect, perhaps, for her business acumen. But as for desire? She'd seen it in his gaze once, twice, when she'd caught him studying her at dinner or over the company records. What would she do married to a man who thought of her as a friend? What she wanted—no, required—was a love that burned and invigorated, that nurtured and enriched. True, she'd glimpsed that only twice. First, between her parents and lately, between her friend, Margaret Alders and her new husband, Vernan Alders.

"I will work to make it so." She had to voice her greatest worry. "But your mother wonders if I have shamed you."

"You and I know that is not so." He caressed her cheek with the warmth of his palm. She tipped her head into his touch, wanting more than this from him. "In your work, you understand truth from fiction. Let that be your guide here with my mother. She does not realize what a diamond you are, my dear. When she sees how happy you make me, she will drop her opposition."

"I'm glad you are certain," she said with more humor than she felt. Indeed, Josephine doubted that the Countess of Stanton understood happiness. The lady was a creature of her noble lineage and the strictures of the *ton*. Bitter, too, though Josephine had no idea why and considered it prudent not to learn.

She sought to turn the somber tone of this conversation. "But I would like it to happen, you see. Certainly before our third child is born."

He chuckled and stepped nearer, drawing her for the first time against his tall firm form. She wound her arms around him, happy for the embrace that she'd yearned for these past few months. Tomorrow, she could do this freely. She went a step more and rested her head against his chest. Beneath her cheek she felt the strong vibrations of his heart. Oh, that she might have that beat for her. Tomorrow and every day henceforth.

The very hope had her pulsing with desire. With her eyes closed, she could see him. Would see him until her last breath. His startling height, his impressive breadth, his coal black hair disheveled on his broad brow as he stood invincible in his portrait upon the dining room wall. He, daring, in his dashing blue jacket with yellow facings, his crimson and gold cords of his busby glowing brightly, the hero who took down the French at Benavente, Lieutenant General the Earl of Stanton of the 10th Regiment of Light Hussars. His face in that portrait was unscarred, without the white line from mid-brow to temple of the blow that gave him headaches and required he use a quizzing glass to improve his sight in that left eye.

He backed away from her, but kept her hand. "Come. I've something to show you."

She could have sworn his bright blue eyes danced, declaring enticing things.

Up the grand main staircase he led her, round and round, to the second floor, down the long hall, past one set of double doors to the end. There he paused before another set.

He opened both wide. "Your suite. Or rather, soon to be."

She gazed upon a sitting room, big as her bedroom in St. James's Square. And nearly empty.

"Furnishings are spare. The two Hepplewhite chairs you may change, of course. The floor needs rugs. Come in here." He led her into the chamber with a door ajar to a smaller room, most likely her boudoir. Here before her stood only a gigantic clothes press and smaller French lingerie chest, both of Rococo design and most likely very old. But there was no bed.

She swung, her mouth open to ask why not.

"I ordered my housekeeper and butler to prepare a list of items the room needed for you. They did, but I must say I failed to choose anything."

"You're busy," she said in quick excuse for him.

"That's not it at all."

"No?" Dare she hope he intended to take her to his bed? Tomorrow night? And all the nights thereafter?

He threw out his arms in frustration. "I did not know what to get for you. What you'd like."

I'd like to sleep with you.

"I want you to have everything you desire."

The lump in her throat grew large.

"I want you to choose. You have excellent taste."

"Do I?" she asked, wistful, charmed and so unaware he had ever noticed any details about her person.

That gave him pause. "I know you do. From the green gowns you favor that turn your eyes to emerald and the pinks that accentuate the blush in your cheeks. You are quite stunning."

No one had ever called her stunning. "Thank you."

He looked at a loss, this man who had commanded hundreds, fought his opponents to the death and who now ran the logistics of supplies that would either make or break the Duke of Wellington's forces against the little Frenchman who would not stay in exile.

She got her wits about her. "I didn't expect you to go to such expense for me."

"Money has no place in marriage. Not in anyone's. Not in ours."

"I agree. And for this, I am delighted to do it." She smiled and spun, arms out, in full circle to welcome the joys of her marriage. Then she went with her impulse and took two steps toward him, and on her tip-toes, reached up to kiss his lips. Briefly. Too briefly.

He clutched her upper arms and as she stepped away, cleared his throat. "I want you to be comfortable. And happy, Josephine."

"As I will work to make you happy, Stanton."

"You'll make me delirious if you use my given name."

She tipped her head to and fro. "I must practice."

"Say it now, then."

"Russell."

He cocked his right brow. "Russ."

She let her eyes dance. "Russ."

"I want this for you, my dear. A completely new start. I owe it to you and to myself. Changing whatever relics of the past that now do not apply to our future."

"I wish to be your loving helpmate."

Once more, he reached out to her and this time, stroked the backs of his fingers down her cheek. "As I will be yours. I am determined to be a good and willing partner, Josephine. Tomorrow I repeat words made by man, meant for God and others. To many who say them, hear them, they are useless. A sign, merely, of lawful commingling. A seal of financial union. I swear to you my words bear none of that. None."

"Nor will mine." *Ever since I first set eyes on you, I have wanted you for my own. Sans title, money, land.*

His sky blue eyes grew stormy with new happiness and old pain. "Hear me, Josephine. Please, as this revelation is new for me. But I will tell you. I do not wish to belabor you with old sorrows but I will have you know this about me. This, which few have ever learned from my lips." He seized a breath. "My first marriage was no union of like minds or pleasures."

He had never spoken of his first wife to her and she doubted to her father, either. While the gossip about the late Countess of Stanton was sparse, the lack of information irritated Josephine especially now that she had accepted his proposal of marriage. A woman who valued an abundance of facts in her work, she knew the past would be vital to understand...and just as vital to avoid duplicating.

He stared at her. "I married my first wife out of duty. Friendship among our families and land that marched beside each other's led to an expectation that she and I marry to seal the union of affections. From childhood, I never questioned it. Neither did Henrietta."

Torment sluiced over his brows and he dropped her hands as if they burned him. Josephine swayed toward him, the magnet of his touch, the hurt of his rejection had always drawn her toward him no matter where he strode.

He took up a stance near the mantel, an Adam's creation of stark white. His severe black dinner attire created a pillar of harsh contrast to the alabaster. His hand to his lips, the swipe of his fingers across his mouth gave her notice that he meant to continue in this dark vein of remembrance.

"Growing up together we thought we knew each other. Certainly we valued the same things, didn't we? The same friends. The Berber horses our fathers raised. The hunt. Poetry." His pause sent a chill up her back and the hair on her arms lifted. "She wanted to marry young and quickly. Her father had died and her older brother had married. She wished to set up her own house. I agreed to that, to everything. I was free. A carefree lad. Randy, actually. And I had the money. Why should I not marry and indulge us both, eh?

"But I did not see that my agreements were one-sided. I wanted the city. She wanted the country. I wanted the work of Parliament and my friends who worked at Whitehall. She wanted the solitude of her dogs and her roses. When I heard the call of the cavalry and the need to defend my country, she did not approve of my decision to join the Hussars. She demanded I return home and give her babies, days of idling in gardens and reading and pulling deadheads from rosebuds."

He ran a hand through his hair. The thick mass rumpled wildly around his aquiline features. "She ordered me not to join, not to leave her alone in the country. I refused. For the next few months, she ran hither and yon about the country. Without word of her whereabouts, she kept me guessing. She also kept the *ton* in ripe gossip. She led me a merry chase. When I learned finally that she had returned home to the Hall, I went there and confronted her. She was wild. She bargained with me. She'd stay in one place if I quit the service and came home to her. She required a constant attendance I could not give her. When I refused, she turned...ugly and took an andiron to me. I bear the scar."

Josephine's mouth fell open. She'd never asked how he'd acquired it, assuming it was a battle scar. "Oh, my dear."

He swung toward her, the horrified look upon his face warning her off. "I left her that night and never returned. I went off to Portugal and Spain, and learned first-hand the delicate art of supplying thousands of men and animals on the march in a foreign land. A year later while I was there, she died of catarrh. I had her buried in her family's crypt. Six years ago, when I returned home to England, I had the Hall in Bury St. Edmonds stripped of all she'd put into it. Since then, I've had a few essential rooms redecorated. That house, too, awaits your kind touch."

He'd told her last week that he'd written to tell staff there that they would arrive at a future date for a wedding holiday and that she would attend to the renovations.

He threw her a wan smile. "When I married her, I was twenty years old. She was eighteen. I thought I knew her. She said we were...cut from the same cloth. Ah, but what does one know at eighteen?"

I knew I loved you. That first afternoon, when my father

brought me into his offices and introduced his friend, the dashing creature who ensured soldiers had uniforms to clothe them, blankets to warm them, beef to sustain them, shot and rifles and cannon and boots.

"I am sixteen years older now, Josephine, and I do hope much wiser. I see in you, my dear, much that resembles my own temperament. You love people and your work, your father and young brother. You see joy in living and cultivate it. I want to make a good husband to you, Josephine, and I promise to give you the best of me."

No declaration of love, but she would take it. "Thank you, Russ. I do not marry you lightly. I've had suitors."

His face broke into a rueful smile. From the looks of it, he welcomed the change to a lighter topic. "I know you have. Many, I would say."

She took his good humor and wished to build on it. "I refused them all."

"Good prospects they were, my darling."

At his use of that endearment, she noted progress in his regard of her. She tipped her head. "You knew, did you?"

He grinned. "Your father and I are very good friends."

She flowed nearer to him, her hands flat to the silk of his waistcoat. "I was never attracted to any of them."

"I often wondered why. They were young. James Caffrey of Hammond Lane was only twenty-five when he asked for your hand three years ago. And what's-his-name English? Thomas English is rich as Midas. Clothier to His Majesty's Army makes him a good catch."

She toyed with a button on his waistcoat. "Youth and money have their charms but I was not enchanted."

"Your father was astonished you refused."

Years ago, he was. Not lately. "Many times, he asked me why. I'm shocked he told you about their proposals."

Russ reached for her, his large sure hands cupping her

cheeks. "Your papa sprinkled details like lures to a treasure. In truth, I heard more from my friends, tidbits of gossip that you would not have any of them. And I rejoiced."

Her heart pounded with his admission. "I wish I'd known."

"Do you?" He hooted, hugged her close and kissed her forehead. "Minx! With every man you refused, I could not keep up with the parade."

"Surely, sir, you can count to five."

He guffawed. "Miss Meadows! Your father counted eight."

"That many? How complimentary!" She wrapped her arms around his waist and drew back to admire the man who would be hers at last. Here in this noble, honorable, hard-working creature was all she had ever desired of love. "I wanted only you."

He blinked, the shock of her declaration making his words sound unrehearsed. "No, surely."

"Most definitely. From the day I strode into Papa's office and he introduced me to you as your personal private accountant."

"Josephine," he pronounced her name as if he were reading a hallowed passage from the Bible. "Sweetheart, you were—"

"Young. But never cloistered. I'd met men, of all ages, for years. In trade, we women are not kept in tidy little confines sipping tea, my darling."

Her statement—perhaps even her own endearment—induced him to crush her close. "You do not marry me because your father wishes it."

"Or because he fears he dies soon. No. I marry you because finally you asked me."

"Josephine—"

"Russell Downey, hear me. I marry you because I want to be your wife."

He gasped and took her lips in a happy declaration of a devotion and yes, a passion that set her on her heels.

He took his lips away all too soon and she nestled into the crook of his shoulder.

He spoke against her ear. "Come. I will accompany you home. I wish to assure your father I am not stealing you away like a highwayman."

She laughed, rejoicing at the results of the evening. "I will always run away with this thief."

"You try a man, my darling. Patience we must have until tomorrow."

She pecked him on the lips. "Tomorrow." She'd almost said, we shall never part. But prudence and his revelations of his first wife cautioned her that binding him to her in any way could resurrect his old torments and destroy all prospects they had for a happy future.

CHAPTER 3

Wednesday, March 28, 1815
No. 16 St. James's Square, London

"That's just so, Sayre." Her father waved away his valet, who put the finishing plump to her father's bed cushions. "I am perfectly situated. You may leave until the ceremony. There you are, Jo, my girl! Come in, come in!"

The overzealous servant contemplated that far longer than most would, then he exited the sitting room and closed the door behind him.

Her father put on a valiant show of strength as he lifted his arm to bid her closer. "What do you think? Am I presentable for this morning?"

"Dashing, I say." Josephine hurried to her father and placed a kiss on his forehead. Sayre had worked his magic, attiring her father in his best linen, a Spitalfields silk maroon waistcoat and grey frock coat, topped with an elaborately tied cravat. What the man could not eliminate were the white lines of pain around Papa's mouth.

"Horse feathers! Not as ravishing as you, my girl."

Her little Blenheim spaniel Rose scampered around her feet, yipping in agreement. She was excellent at imitating the emotions of Josephine and her father.

"Oh, that dog!" Her father made a shooing motion at the creature he adored as much as she. "I hope you're leaving her here for a few days?"

"I am, sir."

"Don't need her in your bed after today," he said in half serious tones.

She pressed her lips together in laughter and shook her head.

"You have better things to do. I told Rodgers to leave you be. And I do hope you repeated that he's to handle all business at least until next Tuesday."

"I did." Fergus Rodgers was her assistant in the company, a trusted employee of her father's for over a decade. Now he was her man. "He agreed only in dire straits would he seek me."

"True. I will keep track of *Aries*."

Their very special cargo on that brig headed from Ostend to the port of Deal was one both of them wanted to monitor. Josephine had given in to her father to relinquish all details of that vessel's arrival for her honeymoon week. Still she was concerned. Their prime Paris agent had sent word via another of their informants last week that she'd sail on their next vessel out of Ostend. The only one due out of that port in the past five days was the *Aries*—and Josephine prayed to God *Madame Argent* made it safely to the ship and to England.

"Ah, ah! Do not scowl at me, girl. Fergus will be on top of this. Now turn around! Around again!" Her father chuckled and began a coughing streak that bent him over in his massive four poster.

"Papa!" She helped to ease him backward to his pillows.

"Let me talk. Water? Tea?"

"Whisky," he croaked.

She'd long since given up casting him a rueful eye over this special palliative, but handed over the glass that was on his night stand. He sipped it slowly, sighed and sank back. A phantom of his former burly self, he nonetheless continued to live in his head. A man of quick mathematical calculations and perceptive geographical computations, he had built his business on his acumen learned in Italian ports. Ten years ago, he'd brought his family to London and opened his business near the East India Docks as a profitable merchandise mart trusted by the Government to service its Army on the Continent.

She glanced about the finely appointed room with ornate plastering and woodwork, the artistry of one of the most noted architects in London. The room, the entire house on the south side of prestigious St. James's Square was a testament to her father's financial success and his understanding of human nature.

He scrutinized her with narrowed eyes. "I like your choice for your wedding. More green than blue, it does justice to your auburn hair. And your mother's pearls in your coiffure. That maid of yours can do miracles. She needs a better pay, what do you think? Stand back. Stand back. Twirl once more. I wish to imprint you on my mind. Like your mother. So like her." He swallowed loudly but the moisture on his lower lids told her of his sweet memories.

"The pearls are a precious gift. I thank you, Papa."

"A young lady needs a memento from her family to help her remember who she is, who loved her first."

"I need no reminders of that. I have lived it with you each day of my life and I am grateful. I take that with me to my marriage, Papa."

"I've no doubt. You were always a good girl, Jo. Smart and wiser than your years. You will do well with Stanton."

The grin that welled up inside her felt glorious.

"I see you agree!" He chuckled and began a new coughing spree.

"Oh, I do not want you to exert yourself!" She helped him to sink once more into his cushions.

"Tell me sour tales then! Happiness makes me laugh." He cupped her cheek. "And I am so happy for you. He is what you want, isn't he?"

"He is."

"More than any other you ever met?"

She arched a wicked brow at him. "More, and well you know it, too!"

"Indeed. For years, I've watched you eye the poor fellow like a starving woman over a tasty treat."

"Oh, you make me sound mercenary." She shushed him and took up the chair near his bed. Arranging her skirts, she pinned him with a testy gaze. "You told him how many proposals I'd had."

He barked in laughter but did not, this time, cough afterward. "An astonishing lot!"

"He didn't need to know!"

"Of course, he did. Any man needs to know his competition."

"None were his competition."

"So I began to realize…"

"Then you do understand that this is no missish infatuation I feel for him?"

"If you'd told me at age eighteen that you had to have him for your own, I would have warned you against him."

"I came to understand that," she admitted.

"He was not a proper mate then for any woman. He had…suffered."

"I had heard rumors, but last night he told me more."

"Good. He is not a man to hide things. But he is discreet, else he would not consult on such dire needs as supplies to France."

"That I detected these past six years you've worked with him. You knew more about him personally than I ever could. And I did not want to be wrong in my choice of a husband." She lifted a shoulder. "If indeed an earl so much more worldly than I would look upon me as…acceptable."

"He bears no prejudices against class."

"That makes him unique among his peers and creates problems for him. Who knows if any of them will accept me? And I would rather live without him than ruin his reputation. But I—"

"What?"

"I am selfish, Papa." She gave a sad little laugh. "You might not think it, but I am."

"I've never seen it in you. How can you say that?"

"Because when he proposed on Christmas, I wanted to wed him that day, that hour. I did not want him to leave or change his mind. I wanted him as I always have and could never refuse him."

He grinned. "Well, then! I would say you are well-mated, my dear child. And I am thrilled for you. Happy for myself, too, that I leave you in the best of care."

A knock at his door had them turning.

"Enter!" he called.

Sayre appeared on the threshold to the bedchamber. "Sir, the vicar has arrived."

"Good! Tell Master Theodore we're ready!" Her brother at fourteen was a keen young man even snappier at maths than she had ever been. He merited a special tutor for his brilliance with algebra and three others for art, architecture and history. "He's to join us now too, Sayre."

Hesitating in the doorway, the valet eyed her father like a bird of prey.

Sayre had strict instructions from her father's physicians not to move him from his bed. Papa had argued repeatedly with his valet and with Josephine, but had succumbed to his own weakness to rise.

"Yes, yes, Sayre. I see your look. I will be docile. Bring the vicar up. Stanton and his family, too, when they get here. No ceremony other than the one we're to embrace, eh?" When the man disappeared, he smiled at her. "Are you ready, Jo?"

She stood and brushed her skirts, nervous, joyful. "Oh, yes, I have been for six years."

~

Stanton House
Grosvenor Square, London

Russ took a last look at himself in his dressing room mirror and assessed the fellow reflected there who would appear to be—as a dandy would say—all the crack. New coat, new waistcoat, new breeches. He snorted. *Daring of you, old man, to fall in love with a young lady who deserves so much better.*

Yet he could not deny how magnetic Josephine Meadows was to his soul. He'd shocked himself when first he admitted to himself he liked her. That had been days after he'd met her six years ago in her father's offices. She was so fresh, so alive that he forced himself to discount his attraction as improper. As years wore on and she continued as his accountant, he wrestled with his admiration for her talents and his delight in her effervescent humor. He told himself he was a satyr who needed a good romp with a woman who knew what she was about in bed—and he'd tried that diversion. To little avail. And here he was marrying her, unable to keep himself from wanting her with him in all ways a man can enjoy a woman.

"You've done me proud, Tipton." He flicked the ends of his cravat and nodded to his valet. "I shall stand up as much younger than my years."

"You *are* young, my lord." His valet—with him seven years now—thought him a self-induced reclusive. The truth was he'd always enjoyed smart company, but only learned to welcome it socially after working with Josephine. "And you deserve her, if I may be so bold as to say."

"You are a jolly fellow, Tipton. And I can be so delighted with the world today that I can even agree I deserve her." *Long may I live to show her what she's done for my belief in the goodness of humans.*

He tugged on the points of his blue and white striped waistcoat. "My frock coat, Tipton."

A minute later, he took the stairs down but halted on the landing.

Forester, his butler, was just closing the front door upon Simpson Walters. His assistant at Horse Guards, Walters had been with him as sergeant in the Hussars and, four years ago, had mustered out with a leg injury. Upon returning home, he'd found Russ at Whitehall and asked for a position. As luck would have it, Russ needed an additional man and he had hired him instantly.

"Forgive me, my lord." Walters worried his hat in his hands. Rain dripped from his hair, his nose, his clothes. He swiped it away. "News from Gravesend. A word, please?

"It's bad. I see it," Russ said when they were sequestered in his library and he'd handed over a generous pour of brandy for his man. "What's wrong?"

"We've had a messenger up from Gravesend this morn. Winds at Deal are blowing hard. The Frigate *Mercurius* and the fleet of transports with it were put back. The *Rosario*, too, with General Lord Hill on board, remains in port."

All had been bound for Ostend, the best port open for troops and supplies since Napoleon had closed Calais and Dunkirk the other day. "Any arrivals from Ostend?"

"Aye, my lord. Two packets yesterday safely in. But another that was due yesterday is in trouble. A lieutenant of the *Templar* out of Bombay says he saw a vessel blown north west, trying to right itself. Its main mast was gone."

"The name of it?"

"In the storm he couldn't see. No wonder. Our runner in Gravesend says that even the huge *Princess Charlotte of Wales*, the outward-bound Indiaman, lost two anchors and cables last night in the gale. So violent it was, she's put back to Deal as well."

Wellington would not be happy with the delay of his rein-forcements for his northern army. At last count, the Duke had thirty thousand men north of Lille, but currently White-hall had no idea how many the French had in their garrison there. The Russians and Austrians who had sent their forces home after Napoleon had abdicated last April, were on the march back, expected to add another one hundred thousand to the fold. Still, they had to hurry.

From Russ's calculations—and information from Josephine's network of spies, they concluded that Napoleon could raise half a million men within two months and put them in arms. That worried Whitehall and they sought news of the Frenchman's recruiting abilities to man his garrisons, especially in the north of France. They did know the emperor lacked sufficient stores of ammunition, uniforms, artillery and especially cavalry horses. Yet the tiresome Corsican was a wily opponent. With one speech he could rally the French to madness.

"Bad news indeed. And the *Aries*?" That supply transport

owned by Meadows Trading Company had sailed last week to Ostend with a cargo of beef, biscuits, gunpowder and tobacco vital to keeping the British Army fed, armed and sane. Returning bound for Deal, *Aries* was ordered to come home brim full of French refugees. "Is she in port?"

"Not yet, my lord. But if she sailed early enough, she might've missed this storm." Walters brushed back his dark wet hair.

"Send our man from Gravesend back to Deal today for news. Hellish weather to keep him out, but can't be helped."

"Yes, sir."

If Fergus Rodgers, Josephine's advisor, had word of this storm and the fate of the *Aries*, he'd run straight to St. James's. Josephine would take it poorly.

He certainly did. This was a bad blow to his hopes for his wedding day. Hers, too.

"Thank you, Walters. Keep me informed."

The man looked skeptical. "My lord, it's your wedding day."

Russ nodded, unable to summon some cheerful statement to console the man or himself.

So much for the adage he'd concocted, to marry at leisure and enjoy at leisure.

Her new husband remained far too quiet in the carriage, rubbing the twitch of his eye as he stared out the window into the gloomy gray day.

"Rethinking your vows already, my lord?" Fortuitously, his coachman paused in the streets, so Josephine rose up and switched sides to sit next to him. Then she took his gloved hand in hers.

He barked in laughter. "Never, my dear wife!" He grinned

96

and pulled off her glove, then kissed the back of her hand. "Forgive my bad humor. Business plagues me."

"I, however, am on holiday from business. May I lure you to do the same?"

"Lure on, Madam!"

Ah well. She had risqué ideas about that, but that should wait, should it not, for tonight?

"Did you enjoy breakfast? I asked Cook to make the fruit-cake of cherries and plums for you." His mother and brother hadn't thought the celebration worthy of remaining for more than the champagne. They'd left soon after the toast to the new couple. "I hope it was as good as your own Cook."

"My dear wife, my Cook is now *our* Cook. And yes, I did enjoy your father's cook's fare. I should be telling you how I enjoyed the entire morning."

"You should indeed." She settled into the sumptuous leather squabs. Everything about this morning's wedding had been deliciously comfortable. The way she'd refused to be offended by Russ's mother's and brother's chilly formalities with her father. The way her husband said his vows with eyes only for her. The way he led her away from others down the hall and whisked her into the small parlor to kiss her at leisure with heat and heart. "So, until you are ready to share your thoughts on our wedding, dear sir, I will tell you how I enjoyed the morning."

"Despite the surliness of my mother."

She bit her lip and let her eyes widen in answer.

He let out a laugh. "And the airs of my brother."

She merely stared at him.

Russ turned her hand over and kissed her palm, a warm generous homage it was, too. "I adore you, Countess Stanton."

Not quite love yet, but she would take this tender bit, too.

"I shall take advantage of your suggestion," he said and

lifted his arm to curl around her shoulders and bring her close. "They've gone now. Not to bother us again until Mama needs money and my brother needs a recommendation to a hatter in Brighton."

She settled into the welcome hollow of his embrace. This was such a good indication of how their relationship might become more amorous. "He does like fashion."

Russ lifted her chin, his gaze encompassing her hat, which he dispensed with and threw to the seat opposite. He chose one loose tendril near her ear and rubbed his fingers down the strands. "I like your hair uncovered. Free. I like the pearls today, too."

She quivered; her breath caught with his compliment. "My mother's. Papa gave them to me yesterday."

"A generous man," he said as he smoothed her hair behind her ear. "I have gifts for you, too."

"Marvelous! When do you give them to me? I am a greedy creature!"

"The devil, you are!" He hugged her close and the whole carriage boomed with his laughter.

"Really I am. When do you give them to me?"

"Tonight."

She took her time letting him see the fullness of her desire for that.

"Scamp!" He kissed her madly on the mouth and she flowed against him, her hand cupping his nape. Gasping, he broke away to trace her bottom lip with his thumb. "Ah, Josephine, I will trade any gifts for kisses like that."

"You don't have to, Russ. I would beggar myself to have yours."

His features fell to desperately decadent lines. "You are the most enchanting woman."

In love with you. She found her voice. "So I needn't sell my wares to gain any kisses?"

"I shouldn't like to bankrupt you."

"Your price, sir!"

"That depends. How many would you like?" he asked, his voice a wreck.

"Innumerable."

"In that case, my darling," he brushed his lips on hers, "let me buy them all."

CHAPTER 4

orester opened the door to them with bright congratulations. Their outer garments dispensed with, he and Josephine stood as the full array of servants lined up for introduction to their new mistress. Josephine had met the butler before and seen a few of the four footmen at service in the dining room, but not met the eight others who served her husband. With a word for each person presented, Josephine offered her promise to all of them that she would be as easy to make happy as their lordship.

"You are such a diplomat, my dear," Russ said as that formality came to an end.

She would have demurred but Forester leaned close to Russ and said, "Sir. Mr. Walters is in the library."

Alarm flashed over his face, but he turned to his wife with a soft smile. "Business, my dear. Forgive me. Come, I'll walk up to the first floor with you. Do continue. I believe your maid arrived earlier, did she not, Forester?"

"She did, sir. My lady, if you wish to refresh yourself, I know your maid has been sorting your wardrobe."

Josephine put a hand to Russ's sleeve when he would have

left her at the landing. "If there is anything I can help with, do summon me."

"I will, darling." He pulled her close and kissed her lips, the warm sorrow in his brief embrace some solace for his necessary departure.

~

His wedding day was not the one to have a disaster at sea! Dammit! He had planned a leisurely afternoon and evening with Josephine. Conversation, reminiscences of childhood, the little revelations about oneself shared with a spouse, dinner and...more. Now, none of that. Not today.

He girded himself for her disappointment. His own was gargantuan, but he had to press on. She would. Yes, she would—and would not take it amiss.

He climbed the stairs to the next floor with anger for the fickle winds of fate that could drive them all to sixes and sevens.

When he opened the doors to his sitting room, he halted. All the air in his lungs drained away. His new wife had been in the process of walking from his bedroom into the sitting room and the light from the far windows shone upon her figure in silhouette. A sylph in diaphanous pearl French silk, his wife paused upon the threshold and his observation of her earthly charms struck him to the quick.

"Forgive me," she said and spun for the bedroom. "I'll return!"

She took a few minutes, long enough for him to encourage a particular part of his anatomy to display much less enthusiasm for hers. Even at that, he worried and found himself taking a chair opposite the fire to cover any tell-tale evidence that might affront her.

When she reappeared, her waist-length hair still flowed

over her shoulders like a cape in the vermilions of a thousand autumn maple leaves. But she'd donned a Ch'ing mandarin-necked forest green brocade dressing gown over the translucent chiffon that was her wedding night gown.

"I took the liberty of ordering supper to be served here. I told them I'd ring when you're ready. But..." She strode closer and brushed the lock of his hair from his brow. Her fingers were an angel's balm to his worries. With solemn ease, she took the chair opposite him and arranged herself as if no shock had occurred to her own system when he saw her nearly... practically...naked. "You've talked with your visitor for over an hour."

Her gaze met his squarely. This before him was his associate, Josephine Meadows. Correction, Josephine Downey, née Meadows, charming woman, beautiful beyond mere words, able to add long columns of numbers or nautical distances, sans ink and paper. "Whatever it is, it's bad, isn't it?"

There was no sugar-coating the problems. "Terrible."

She tipped her head and folded her hands serenely in her lap. "What can you tell me?"

This was the twenty-four-year-old who bought beef on the hoof for the Army barracks here in country and who recalled precise ballast loads better than he. Here before him sat the current head of Meadows Trading Company, that entity now thirty-two years in business, with offices in London, Deal and Dover. Thirty-two years ago, her father had opened his business with a partner out of Genoa. They had developed an extensive network of correspondents throughout the Mediterranean and regularly fed information to the British espionage agents. Meadows had come to the attention of Whitehall seventeen years ago when he relayed intelligence that the French were loading particular types of barrels at Leghorn. Such items were useful only if ships needed to traverse shallow waters. Whitehall saw that this meant Napoleon would invade Egypt and they sent Sir Horatio Nelson to harry the little man. In one stroke, Meadows not only had helped destroy Napoleon's dreams of empire in Africa, but secured his own place in Whitehall's intelligence network.

When Josephine assumed total control over the company four months ago, she assured Whitehall of her continuing dedication to delivering covert information to the Government. While Russ was not directly involved in her company's espionage information—nor did he ask or need to be, he coordinated efforts with her and benefitted in his own work from her network's excellent source of information. She had agents in Paris—one *Madame Argent* very well placed—who provided her and him with detailed numbers. This included such vital statistics as those numbers of soldiers under arms, rioters in the streets, the defenses of northern French garrisons...and even how much gold the little French despot had to spend on recruiting reluctant Frenchmen to sign up for his infantry.

Russ trusted her implicitly with everything. News of troops and transports. Facts about his unpleasant first marriage. And now, even his heart. But this disturbing news, on their wedding night, riled him to tell her. "We've got a troop transport out of Portsmouth run afoul by a brig that stove in her bows. The bowsprits broken, too. She's leaking. A hundred or more troops injured. Fourteen crew dead."

She stared at him, painstakingly assessing the damage. "You must go."

~

CERISE DELAND

Less than an hour later, she kissed him goodbye with all the resolve of a businesswoman and the sorrow of an hours'-old bride.

He cupped her cheek. "I'll meet with the Prime Minister at Whitehall and return as soon as I can."

"And I await you in there." She tipped her head toward his bedroom.

He pressed her tightly into his embrace and rocked her. "Forgive me this departure."

She did, of course, excuse him all. But as the hours ticked by, she rued her loss of her groom. Not much served as substitute, however. Though supper was filling. The wine smooth. The brandy smoother. Alone, none of it had any taste. After that, she told Jane to go to bed.

The fire in the grate was high. The night was cold and chilly though the rain outside had stopped. But storms in the Channel were nothing new. Nor were stories of ships tossed by them, but with so much at stake in this new assault against Napoleon, she was disheartened.

She sighed, wishing she'd brought her little dog with her. Or even her work. She'd left her ledgers of yesterday's arrivals locked in her desk in her office in St. James's. Perhaps a book! An adventure! She'd begun one last week titled *Waverly* by some man with an impossibly funny name of Jebediah Cleisbotham.

Sliding her hand across the cold marble of the mantel, she admitted to herself she was taken aback by the change in her wedding night. She'd hoped for a delightful evening, a consummation of all her years of yearning for the noble Earl of Stanton. Unafraid and welcoming the physical joining of him to herself, she pushed back the disappointment that made her frown and ponder how and when she might become his wife in deed as well as word.

Idle now, she trailed her fingertips over the ormolu

French clock on the mantel and the Murano glass vase on the sideboard. She was never idle, without a task, a project, a job to do. On this wedding night she had planned to enjoy herself. Alas.

She roamed her husband's bedchamber, searching it in detail for him. He was everywhere. In the sturdy masculine mahogany linenfold paneling of his dressing room. In the careful white muslin drape in his toilette room. In the handsome wainscotting of his master closet. The fragrance of his lime and anise cologne hanging in the air. The precise march of his boots and shoes across the racks. His superfine frock coats hanging from molds, the breadth of those shoulders no match for the symmetry of his body and the lure of his embrace.

She touched one coat, the wool a silken texture that sent her away in search of anything to distract her from the sorrow of being alone on this of all nights.

She plunked into the overstuffed chair and sat to dream of the company she missed tonight. Next to the chair upon the table sat a book of poetry.

She picked it up and opened it to the page he'd marked by the leather band. She grinned. Her husband might be a tower of integrity and restraint, a force to be reckoned with in the Government, but he evidently had taken to reading the love poetry of that noted cavalier, Andrew Marvell. The words of *To His Coy Mistress* had her chuckling.

Who would have thought her rational, stoic-looking husband would like this?

> *And now, like am'rous birds of prey,*
> *Rather at once our Time devour,*
> *Than languish in his slow-chapt pow'r.*
> *Let us roll all our Strength, and all*
> *Our sweetness, up into one Ball:*

> *And tear our Pleasures with rough strife,*
> *Thorough the Iron gates of Life.*
> *Thus, though we cannot make our Sun*
> *Stand still, yet we will make him run.*

She let the book drop to her lap. Watching the flames dart behind the grate, she vowed that, when she had the chance, she would do her part to make her husband's Sun stand still.

She needed a different book. Anything to divert her. Help her fall asleep. The *Orations of Cicero* would keep her awake. She'd admired Caesar's *Gallic Wars*, but not the old bombastic Roman orator.

She made her way down the winding staircase to the first floor and had just gained the library when she heard a pounding at the front door. She paused, listening to the footman who was on night watch tonight rattle the locks and grumble at the untimely intrusion. Voices floated up the stairs. A man called and he sounded worried, urgent. She hastened down the hall. The servant took the steps up. As he turned the landing for the second floor, she gained the top of the staircase.

"I say, Barns?" She wrapped her dressing gown closer about her. "It is Barns, isn't it? Do you wish to speak to me?"

"Aye, milady. A caller for you."

After ten at night? Not a good sign. "Who is it?"

"Says 'is name is Rodgers."

Fergus? Her man was not to bother her tonight. Yet here he was. "I will see him. No need to bring him up. I will go down." Whatever had driven her man here would not wait on ceremony.

Nor did he. She barely reached the bottom step when he said, "I come from St. James's, Miss. Er...my lady. I went straight there, I did."

She waved a hand. "Do not worry about formalities, Rodgers. You saw my father?"

"Asked for 'im, I did. Woke him. He told me to come. Sorry, milady, but—"

"It's serious. Yes. What is it?"

"We've our runner up from Deal." Runners dashed up from the coast on a regular basis to alert her and her staff to arrivals, departures and those plans that changed for whatever reason. Only a disaster would compel Rodgers to her so late at night. And with the approval of her father on this auspicious evening, too.

"And? His news? Is it the storms in the Channel?"

"Aye, milady. Our sloop out of Newcastle, bound for Ostend, had to change course and put in at Deal midday. Blown off, she was. No mizzen, ye see. Takin' water."

"Men lost?" That was the worst when men died. Meadows Trading hired on seasoned sailors, paid them well, so when they lost men, they lost the finest.

"No'm. They didn't. But Captain Torrens tells he saw our *Aries* in distress off the coast of Yarmouth. Listing, she was. He couldn't see the main mast what with storm ragin' so hard."

"The *Aries* was bound home out of Ostend." *Aries* was a brig the Company ran usually between Deal and Calais, but she had changed her destination last week after Napoleon threatened all ships landing in French Channel ports. For her special trip, *Aries's* captain strained crew and craft to get into Ostend with precious cargo and out swiftly. This trip she had priceless cargo from Ostend. Meadows Trading Company's prime agent in Paris.

"She was, Miss."

Josephine had dealt with crises similar to this. Ships blown off course, especially in the Channel or North Sea, were not uncommon. Most survived, even if they came in to port damaged.

"Any other of our arrivals delayed?" She had to know the full of the current problem. The fate of her Paris agent was a horrifying mystery, which said nothing of the fate of the other passengers on board, most of them refugees from Napoleon. If her agent were lost now with that woman's most vital information, Josephine did not know how she would rightly calculate new quantities of beef and boots and gunpowder for the Allies.

"None, milady. All due in are safely in."

"Thank you, Rodgers. Have you had supper?" He was a tall, strapping man of thirty or more but he shivered like a child in this raw weather.

"No, milady."

She went to the bell pull. "I'll have the butler show you to the kitchen. You eat before you go. I assume my father sent you here in one of his carriages?"

"Aye, he did, ma'am."

"Good. You'll take it to the office and tell our runner—" She frowned, her mind awhirl with plans of how to learn about the fate of the *Aries* and all aboard. "Tell everyone, I'm for Yarmouth. Any future word of *Aries*, then you send a man north to me."

He did not argue. He knew better. What Josephine decided, she never wavered from.

She ran a hand through her hair, estimating travel times from London to the north east town of Yarmouth. "I'll be at Stanton Hall in Bury St. Edmonds by tomorrow sometime, depending on weather. Then I press on to Yarmouth. I must discover what happened to the *Aries*."

CHAPTER 5

*H*e arrived home after two, chilled of mind and body. His hat, coat and walking stick turned over to the night footman, he went for the stairs and his new wife.

But his man interrupted him. "My lord, Lady Stanton is not at home."

"What?" An old pain sliced through him. His eye twitched. Silly, he thought himself done with women who fled suddenly in the middle of the night. Like ghosts. Like a particular ghost, this was. But reason countermanded old fears. "Why? Her father? Is he not well?"

"I dunno, sir. One of her men come to call earlier. Roberts or—?"

"Rodgers? Yes." That man was her assistant. If her father had taken a poor turn, a servant from St. James's would have come to fetch her. That she'd gone because of business eased his woes. Yet, because of what he'd been through tonight with transports lost and men dead, his worries doubled. The hideous storms in the Channel and North Sea had been brutal. "And? What?"

"They talked. He left, she dressed, then she called for the brougham, my lord. She said to tell you she had to see her father."

"How long ago?"

"Just after ten o'clock. But Bagby came home about an hour ago, sir. She sent him. Told him to go to bed."

"Did she say how long she'd be?"

"No, sir. Gave him a letter for you, she did."

"Do you have it?"

"I put it upstairs in your sitting room, sir."

He took the stairs at a run.

By noon the next day, Josephine sat fretting as her Meadows coachman and groom attempted to roll the heavy coach from yet one more muddied lane. Though the rain had stopped over an hour ago, her servants would not let her, her maid or her dog Rose out while they struggled. A six-hour ride had become ten.

She huddled in her winter wool coat, glad she'd seen fit to wear it. The early morning ride out of London had proven bone-chilling. The roads northeast were so drenched that she might have considered swimming to Yarmouth. Her little dog, Rose, snuggled into her blankets on the backward-facing seat, sleeping through the occasional downpours and the endless gut-wrenching ruts in the roads. Not so for Josephine's maid, Jane. The poor girl who was ever valiant had climbed into the Meadows's traveling coach last night with her at one o'clock, bleary-eyed. The deluge had not improved her spirits and judging from her cough, not done anything for her worsening health, either.

"When we make the Hall, I want you to remain there, Jane."

"No, Ma'am. I will na."

"You cannot come. Your health is more important than you accompanying me."

"Lord Stanton and your father will turn me out if I do na go."

"And I will hire you back. Rest. Do not worry," she said and the maid took her word and settled back into her uneasy slumber.

Josephine eyed the gun case beneath the opposite seat. She had her blunderbuss and her skills with it. Her Meadows coachman had his larger one. Although it was up underneath his seat, she doubted the powder in it was dry enough to fell a mouse. In her own valise, she had packed her own tiny muff pistol. A French affair with Sèvres china handle and gold trim, the weapon was one of a pair her father had bought from a French comte whose estates and income were lost to him in the Terror. His family executed by the guillotine, the man now sought to become a proper Englishman.

Those who had stayed in France to embrace the new Republic, changing their allegiances to retain what rights they had to land and their homes, had found it just as hard going. That included her *Madame Argent,* as they called her in the Company. *Madame Silver*, her best agent, close to the Bourbon court, was just as trusted among the Bonapartes. For the past five years, even through the Bourbon Restoration and now the Bonapartist, *Madame* had obtained the most sensitive and reliable information about everything from the restored king's gluttonous diet to the numbers of soldiers in various regiments. How the woman managed such a transition from *ancien regime* to republican to Bonapartist was unimaginable—and invaluable to Whitehall.

The lady was an asset whose worth Josephine could not count so much in British lives saved as in the guessing games the British did not need to play. Expediting *Madame Argent*'s flight from Paris on short notice had been easy. Perhaps too much so. She'd simply declared her intentions, sent word through the network, learned of Meadows ships lately leaving Ostend and headed there. Josephine knew not how, but simply that they had to find her. If she were on the *Aries*, she had to hide her away from the man who years ago had put a bounty on her, mystery as she was to them. Joseph Fouché, Napoleon's chief of Police, was not known to leave off pursuit of an enemy whose life and activities he wished to extinguish.

Josephine shifted, uneasy, as she gazed at the whirling grey clouds. She fought not to think of Russ, wondering how he'd taken her scribbled note telling him of her departure. Her apology for leaving on their wedding night. She hoped that he imbibed the urgency of her mission in her clipped words. He did not know much about *Madame Argent*. The fewer who knew, the better. He, like Josephine, did not know her real name, her home or what her connections were to Republicans and Imperialists alike. He knew that she had been her father's agent before Josephine's—and that all of the woman's information had been of incalculable value.

With hopes *Madame* was alive, that if she'd sailed on the *Aries,* that it too survived, Josephine meant to save the woman and the vital bits of intelligence she could relay in this last desperate fight against the little emperor they had to defeat.

∼

Stanton Hall
Bury St. Edmonds

Russ climbed down from his traveling coach and hurried into the foyer.

"Bloody weather, Firth." He pulled off his gloves, then handed over his hat, coat and walking stick. With a hand through his disheveled hair, he glanced about the serene Wedgwood blue and white foyer. This country home was one he rarely visited these past few years. He'd been too busy in London. As a boy, he had loved the house, the rolling fields, the forests thick and dark, the solitude away from his feuding parents. "Sorry to rush in on you without warning."

"To have you with us, milord, is never an inconvenience. We had fair warning you'd follow when Lady Stanton arrived yesterday."

"Is she here?" He didn't expect her to tarry here, but one could never predict travel times during inclement weather.

"No, sir. She left us this morning." His butler here in this house had been with his family since Russ could remember. Once the major domo in his London house, Reginald Firth and his wife Maribel, the housekeeper, had retired here more than nine years ago. They kept it up to snuff, and he had every right to believe that they had responded to the surprising arrival of the new Countess of Stanton with an aplomb indicative of their years of service. "She was bound for Yarmouth, sir."

"Yes. I know."

Firth looked relieved at that. The butler had known Russ's first wife, who'd appear at odd times and hie off here or there, never having told Russ or the staff where she'd gone or when or why.

"What time did she leave?" He had to estimate her arrival in Yarmouth. He wanted to be there for support if news of her agent's survival were bad.

"After eight, my lord."

"Early, that."

"Yes, sir. She wanted to leave earlier but that Meadows coach of hers is in disrepair. Problems with the wheels. Her coachman and groom are ill. Took a deep chill, they did. Her maid, too."

"And my wife?" Russ had never known Josephine to take cold, but there was always a first time. "Is she sick too?"

"No, sir. Not that I could see. Hardy lass."

"Yes. Very. So if the Meadows coach is down, how did my wife travel?" He hoped to God she hadn't attempted to ride. Nor to go without a groom.

"She had us order a hack from town."

Not the most comfortable conveyance. Still. "She's alone?"

Firth gave him a smile. "With Billy James up in the box, sir."

The James family had run the best stables and smithy in Bury for generations. "Ah. A good man."

"She took her little dog, too, my lord."

He had to smile. "Rose."

"Sir?"

"The Countess's spaniel."

"Happy little bit."

"She is, until she comes upon a man she does not like." Then she barks until he is removed from her sight.

The old butler drew his hoary brows together. "Mayhaps then she's a good protector."

"Indeed." *And I will join her in that effort.* "Hot coffee for me, Firth. Porridge or stew. Something bracing from the kitchen for my coachman and groom, too. Then we're off. But first, where is the Countess's maid?"

"Upstairs sleeping in milady's dressing room."

"Come. Awaken her for me. I wish to speak with her

briefly." He motioned for the butler to precede him up the stairs. "And the maid's name? Refresh my memory, Firth."

"Jane, sir."

*Y*esterday's rain had gone but thunder still threatened. Lightning danced along. The horses spooked at the harsher bolts, but kept to the road.

Josephine hated to keep Billy James on the cold harsh task, but what alternatives did she have? She had made a commitment to preserve and protect Papa's network and for this, his finest asset, this woman who had brought them word of the decisions of Napoleon's councilors since long before his abdication, she could not fail.

The coach slowed.

Rose raised her little head and sniffed the air. If they were encountering anyone, Rose would tell her mistress whether they were friend or foe just by the smell of them.

Josephine clutched her little pistol, insurance against chaos.

Billy James rapped on the roof. "Road's under water, ma'am. Slow going, 'ere. But a farm's ahead. I'll ask about them's that's docked. I can see two brigs anchored off to sea. Royal Navy I bet. Hard goin' in this." She'd told him she had to learn the fate of a certain ship. He'd accepted her explanation for continuing her journey in such foul weather.

"Ask whomever you meet if they've heard or seen the ship *Aries*."

He led them around a bend and stopped before an old grey stone cottage.

Josephine overheard his conversation with the woman which, according to their raised voices, did not progress well. She was testy. James was persistent, asking what she knew of ships and road conditions.

He ran to the coach and pulled the door ajar, his jolly round face nearly obscured by the bulk of his knitted scarf. "No new ships docking in past two days, she says. But two shipwrecks, she told me, ma'am. On the coast, near the church, she says there's an inn."

"Good! Let's put in there, if they've room. Did she know if there are survivors of the wrecks?"

"I didn't ask."

"Still we must go and get out of this chill!"

"Aye, ma'am. Not far."

When he pulled into the courtyard of a tumble-down inn, Josephine checked her pocketwatch. It was only four-twenty but the grey storm clouds made it look like nine or ten at night. They could go no further tonight. But James was jovial still when he stopped the hack and yanked open her door.

A quick glance at the far cluster of cottages told her the village had seen better days. So had the half-timbered inn. A sign dangling from precarious straps flapping to and fro in the sharp wind denoted this was The Queen's Barque.

Josephine hopped down, Rose under one arm, and pressed money into her coachman's hand. "A bit extra for you and your kindness to me on this journey. You keep this."

"Thank ye, ma'am."

"I do see the inn has a stables and a coach house. Please

get rest and refreshment for yourself and the horses. I pay for it all."

"Aye, ma'am. Yer kind. I'm off to it!" He handed over her little valise to the tall thin fellow who came running to greet them.

The sprawling establishment spoke of the past glories during the reign of the Tudors. As Josephine hurried inside and up the stairs, the place looked clean. On the first floor, the inn opened up to a gathering room and a huge bar. By wafts from flames in the huge fireplace, she was instantly warmed. A giant dog, a hulking mastiff with odd floppy ears bounded up to her, sniffing Rose. Her little pet regarded the huge mutt with a dainty sniff of disdain followed by a wag of her tail.

"Hector! Off with you!" The man who carried her bag threw Josephine a smile. "Mister Brewster, at your service, ma'am. The Queen's Barque, about to be restored to greatness."

If that was so, Josephine applauded his ambition for the inn needed as much money as skill to renew her faded beauty.

"A meal? A room, ma'am?"

"Yes, thank you, sir. Your best room with a fireplace, if you have it." From the corner of her eye, she saw a few people in a common room huddled near the big hearth. The aromas from the kitchen to her right made her faint with hunger. "I see you've a full establishment. I would ask for a beer here in the gathering room, if that's possible, within minutes."

"Of course, Ma'am. Your name, ma'am?"

She leaned close to him, discretion appropriate for her mission. "I am Lady Stanton." So odd it seemed to say that, when in many ways, she was not yet that particular person.

"Milady." He shifted her valise to his other hand and

pulled his forelock. "Come with me." He led her up the main stairs to the bedrooms. "We've not had so many in our inn for years. Happy to. Happy to. We've even a gent from London. One of our maids—Alice, she is—says he writes for a London newspaper. I told her to suggest to him that he write about our inn. Bring more visitors, you see, and make us well known. Rich, too."

"Really? How nice." Her feet were frozen. When that happened to her, a chest congestion was not far behind.

"Alice says he told her he's here to catch flies and spies."

Horrified, she gasped, then quickly covered it with a short laugh. "How amusing." It damn well wasn't, but she could not agree with such a truthful concept as that. "I understand this storm has brought damaged ships to your shores."

"Aye, ma'am. Limping into the harbor, they are. We've had to drag up from the beach more'n eight poor souls gone overboard."

"Eight?" Her heart skipped a beat.

"Four of 'em dead. Drowned."

"Oh, that's awful. Awful. And...and the others?"

"Others?" He opened the door to a simple but serviceable room with rough-hewn wooden bed, wash stand, cupboard and screen.

"Yes. The other four? Do they still live?"

He scratched his head. "Far's I know, ma'am. They're lying in an old wing. Our vicar tends 'em. Had his start setting bones and so on."

"I see. I see. Are they cogent?"

He frowned. "Co—?"

"Awake? Aware?"

"Not sure. You'd have to ask him. Our vicar, that is."

"Where is he?" She had no experience dealing with delirious patients. And she had to admit now that she was here, she felt a twinge of fear. But she had to march on, didn't she? So much depended on *Madame* and what information she brought with her of Napoleon's readiness for battle.

"He was downstairs a few minutes ago. Talked to my wife, he did."

"I'd appreciate an introduction, if you would, sir."

"I can." He assessed her with narrowed eyes. "You think you know these castaways, do you?"

What to say? Yes? And give herself away? No? And sound like some ghoul who liked looking upon those afflicted by nature and God? "I'd like to help him."

"Ah, well. There you are!" He went for the door. "Come down when you can. I'll get your supper out for you. Beer, too."

"Thank you. And for my coachman, also, please give him whatever he wishes."

"He'll be with the others then in the stables and sleep in the loft. We'll provide well for him, we will."

"Thank you. His name is James. Billy James."

"Right you are, my lady. Right you are."

"Sir? On second thought. If you would put out a pitcher of beer or wine for me to take up to the survivors right away. I'll take them that and water, bandages. Supper, too."

"Aye, my lady. Good of you. Come along when you're washed, eh? I'll give you goods to take to 'em."

"I will reimburse you for your kindnesses to them, Mister Brewster."

"That's good of you, my lady."

"We must help each other in crises, shouldn't we?"

Russ climbed down from his traveling coach and made his way across the courtyard.

From the looks of The Queen's Barque Inn, she'd stood much too long against the winds of time and fortune. In the gloom of a charcoal-covered sky, the rough and tumble building stood along a shore dotted with a lonely church and a few farm houses.

"Milord." A tall fellow rushed out to greet him and flung a towel over his shoulder. He was squinting, trying to read the family escutcheon on the side of his carriage. "Honored to have you."

Russ nodded to the man whom he presumed was the proprietor. Peeling off his gloves, he scanned the steps up to the first floor of the big inn. Old it might be, but inside a welcome warmth flowed around him.

"Come upstairs, milord." The man beckoned. "We're happy to have you."

Russ would be happiest if his wife was here. His coachman had questioned a matron on the coach road who told of ships in distress, damaged, shipwrecks and passengers and crew floating in to shore. "I understand yours is the only inn on the shore?"

The innkeeper paused at the entrance to the gathering room where dozens milled about. "We are, milord."

"Do you have here—?" Russ caught a glimpse of a figure in heavy purple wool descending the stairs, the only sight he'd ever wished to see here or anywhere else in this world or next. "My wife."

He opened his arms wide.

Josephine rushed to him, one arm going around his shoulder, the other clutching a squirming ball of white and red fur.

"My darling," he whispered and lifted her chin, beside himself to kiss her here, to hell with propriety. "You look well."

"I am. About to be even better thanks to Mister Brewster's hospitality, too." She pressed her fingers into his forearm, looking here and there, aware they made a bit of a scene. "But I am even happier now that you're here."

He hugged her close, damn the rules. Laughing at the wiggling dog between them and the enormous white muff she held, he nonetheless was able to plant a kiss on her sweet lips. "I had to come."

In her eyes stood tell-tale tears. "I began to regret that I wrote you must not follow me."

"My dear wife, why would I stay away? This is our honeymoon!"

She let her head fall back as laughter shook her to her core. "Oh, how I love you!"

"Do you, darling?" His heart left his chest. Worth riding to the ends of the earth to hear that from her.

"I have loved you for eternities."

That—he caught his sanity—was more than he'd hoped for. In the beauty of her forest green eyes, he saw all the verification he'd ever hoped to have of this, his wife's affections. He'd planned to reveal his own ardor in an appropriate moment on their wedding night. To declare it now would seem like mere reciprocity and the love he bore her was no trifle meant to be tossed at her in exchange for her own heart-felt declaration. He drew her closer, detecting in her body's reaction no slight at his failure to proclaim his affection. His Josephine had declared who she was, what she felt. He would treasure it and her for eternity, and save his own words of devotion for a time and place more intimate than this.

"Oh, Russ." She flowed against him, her expression full of the devotion he'd longed to see she had for him, to the devil with anyone in that room. "I have never loved you more than now that you've come to help me."

He cupped her cheek and brushed his thumb across her

tempting lower lip. Dear God, he loved this woman. "I will always stand by you. In this. In all else."

She fought back tears.

He dug out a handkerchief from his greatcoat pocket and handed it to her. "Have you a room?"

"Yes. I arrived only minutes ago." She dabbed at the corners of her eyes. "The hack. The coachman was so kind. Persevering as no other. The rain and the roads are hideous."

"I know. I was happy when Firth told me you'd hired Billy James. I knew he'd take good care of you."

"Milord?" The proprietor had been cooling his heels while they reunited. "Supper for you?"

"Thank you, yes. Beer too." He took Josephine's arm and wound it through his.

She pulled him close, her green eyes suddenly hard with serious intent. "Would you mind, my dear, if you and I had our supper later? You see, there are poor souls who are survivors of shipwrecks up in another part of the inn."

"I see," he said, reading the purpose in her features. "And we should go help them, shouldn't we?"

She hugged his arm and planted a kiss on his cheek. "We must. Mister Brewster is kind enough to give us supper for them. Do they—?" She turned to the proprietor. "Do they need clean bandages? Blankets? What else might we take to them?"

"I think they have enough blankets. Bandages, no need of, as far as the vicar has said. But supper? Aye, hot food'll do them right. I'll have one of my daughters bring out a pot. Hot, it'll be. She should carry it up. Bowls. And water."

"I told Mister Brewster we would be paying for the care and feeding of the castaways."

"Indeed, we will," Russ added. "If you've any wine, that, too, sir."

"Aye, milord. Ours is not the finest but you'll find it

surprisingly good." He tipped his head toward the gathering room. "If you'll take a seat there, I'll get the kitchen to gather it all."

When they were seated at the wooden trestle in the far corner near the fire, he took her cold hand in his. "What do you know of your ship and your passenger?"

"Go play, Rose." She let her spaniel romp with a huge old dog that looked like a cross between a mastiff and a hound. Then she told him all she knew.

At the end of her tale, her lips quivered. "You're not angry that I left home on our wedding night?"

He hugged her against him. "Steady on, my darling. I read your note and immediately understood and agreed. We will see to this matter first and then have forevermore to see to our marriage, eh?"

She broke then, putting her face to his shoulder and letting out her frustration with her silent tears.

He could not care about the audience they had. She sought him. She needed him. She loved him.

And he now had to help her complete this hideous challenge of learning the fate of her agent. That might be here or in Yarmouth or another town, another shore.

But after that, in all good faith, he would declare that she was and would always be the love of his life.

CHAPTER 7

hey finished their beer just as one of Brewster's daughters appeared with a cast-iron pot in one hand and a pitcher in the other. Behind her stood a maid, the one they called Alice. She was shorter and thinner than the hearty Brewster girl and carried four earthen bowls and a pitcher full of spoons. But she had a newspaper crammed in her pocket and her gaze darted everywhere noting all the details of the room. Plus her fingers were ink-stained. Did she spend her leisure hours writing? Odd for a maid to be so well educated that she devoted herself with such endeavors. He'd find time later to visit with her and commend her for her writing.

Russ rushed to the Brewster's girl's side and reached for the handle of her stew pot and her thick old mitt. "I'll carry that for you, Miss."

She gave it over with a smile. "But you must know that some aren't eating or drinking. Too sick."

"We'll offer it all anyway," Josephine said.

The Brewster daughter lead the way through dark narrow corridors. She raised high a candlestick, Josephine behind her, followed by the other Brewster girl. Each held a candle. Russ came last, Rose scampering up the steps behind him.

The chamber was old, small but cozy and their candles gave a soft illumination to three bodies laid out around the edges of the room, all covered in old blankets. A fourth, a woman in rags, sat slumped on a bale of hay, one arm in wooden splints. As Russ met her gaze, he detected her fevered state. A glance at the others told him two more were women and the other, a man. If those three slept or suffered from unconsciousness, he was not clear.

"*Bonjour, Madame,*" he greeted the woman.

"Good day," she responded in refined English, suitable for any London drawing room.

Rose scampered up to her, sniffed her hands and feet, then circled the other survivors on the floor. The male did not appeal to her because she sat at his feet and barked sharply at him. He did not respond.

"Quiet, Rose!" Josephine admonished the dog. "Sit!"

The animal whined but sank to the wooden floorboards with a huff, her nose twitching near the man's bare feet.

Russ approached the lady with the splint. "Allow me to introduce myself."

She coughed and waved an impatient hand at him and Josephine. In the dim light and in her disheveled condition, he could not detect her complexion or the whites of her eyes. Nor could he say how old she was or how healthy or disabled other than sight of her broken bone.

"I am Lord Stanton and this is my wife."

"Good of you." Her voice was a rasp. "I am Emily Norton. Mrs. Trenton Norton, of Norton and Stokes, formerly of Chantilly."

Russ smiled politely, noting she claimed her home was

that small town north of Paris. Had she sailed on the *Aries*? Might she be *Madame Argent*?

"Oh, ma'am!" Josephine took her limp hand in her own, solicitous for the woman's infirmity. "I am the owner of Meadows Trading Company. My father has spoken often of you and your husband. You deal in French fabrics and lace."

The lady gave Josephine a weak smile. "My, my. Meadows. Odd. Fate is odd, eh? I remember your father. Met you once when you were ten or...eleven? Where were we? Genoa? Can't remember. Can't. But oh, you do look like your mother, you do."

"You knew her?" Josephine grinned at the news. "Marvelous! Oh, Ma'am, we're here to help you return home. My husband and I are so horrified to hear of your travails at sea."

"What's your given name? Joan? Jean?" The lady coughed but leaned forward to examine Josephine more closely.

She told her.

"Ah, yes. The bright child. The one who added numbers in her head." She coughed again, fighting a deeper liquid disturbance in her lungs.

Russ knelt before her. "You've a broken arm?"

She let Josephine feel her brow. "Lucky I don't have more, eh?"

"Are you hungry? Thirsty?" Russ motioned for one of the young girls to approach.

"Yes. Thank you. I'd like that, I would."

"Mrs. Norton." Josephine stoked her hand. "Tell us what happened to you. And if you know, what of these three, too."

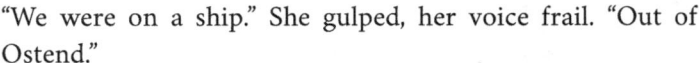

"We were on a ship." She gulped, her voice frail. "Out of Ostend."

Russ directed the Brewster girl to pour water into an earthen mug and gave it to Mrs. Norton.

"The name of it?" Russ asked.

She sipped the water. "*Aries.*"

"Oh, ma'am." Josephine burst with delight followed by dread at her revelation. "Is it sunk?"

Her eyes told tales of nightmares beyond her ability to describe. "Oh, yes. We were struck by lightning and the ship listed. It was... I swear to you I've no idea how I'm here. Or you, for that matter." She coughed, bent over with the force of it.

Josephine asked for a mug of wine. "Try this. It will soothe your throat. We should get her warm brandy, Russ. That will help."

The woman waved her quiet and pressed a hand to her throat. "Listen to me. All on *Aries* are gone."

"All?" Josephine wanted to scream at the possibility. "Are these three not from the *Aries*?"

"We four? Yes. But others?" She shook her head, weary. "Gone. There were others here...I think. Six? I do not recall."

Josephine realized the lady was confused. Understandable in the circumstances. "Yes, Mrs. Norton, there were other survivors but they've died."

"Nooo." The woman sagged with grief. "When?"

"I'm not certain," Josephine told her and stroked her good hand. "The innkeeper told me there were four more who washed up here. Did you see them come ashore?"

The woman shook her head, but gazed around the room as if she might suddenly find the others sitting there. "Four more? I cannot be sure."

"Might you have known any of those onboard who survived or—?"

"My maid," the woman said and tears sprang to her eyes.

Russ handed her his handkerchief.

She took it eagerly, wiping her cheeks. "She was a good girl. Very good."

"I am so sorry, Mrs. Norton." Josephine knew how dear a servant could become. "Do you have family in England? Anyone you can go to?"

One of the women stirred upon the floor, moaning and curling into a ball of misery.

"My sister in Brighton," Mrs. Norton went on and wiped her nose. "I've not seen her in four years."

"Have you been abroad all that time?" Josephine asked, nonchalant about her question.

The woman's red-rimmed eyes narrowed on Josephine, her demeanor at once wary.

Russ stiffened.

"I have," she said simply and for a moment, pressed her lips together.

Had she said something wrong? Russ noted she did not elaborate on where she'd lived during that period. Certainly, an Englishwoman in trade could not have been in Chantilly for four years. Not in her role as yard goods merchant. Yet the woman was not volunteering the information that would clear the cloud from her name. Nor should she. Not to someone she'd met minutes ago.

Russ took the woman's mug from her, giving no indication of his concern about her revelation. "Let me give you more."

Josephine pointed to those upon the floor. "Do you know these three persons, Mrs. Norton?"

Russ wrapped the woman's shaking hands around the mug of red wine.

"Them?" She drank, much too quickly and coughed. When she had her breath, she pointed at the man. "Not him."

"And the ladies?"

"Sad, those two." She stared at the two bodies curled up

into ragged woolen blankets on the hay strewn floor. "I'm shocked they still live."

"What?" Josephine gazed at the two who faced each other. The younger one who moaned had stopped but her eyes were now open. "Why?"

"They argued like cats and dogs from the minute we left Ostend."

"Did they travel together?"

Russ noted that their soiled and torn attire told him little of their status.

Mrs. Norton frowned over that. "Probably."

"Do you know their names?"

"That one," she said as she pointed to the older woman, a silver blonde who struggled to breathe, "is Madame. Madame la Duchesse, that one called her."

Russ looked more closely at the duchess. *Madame* meant nothing of any import. Josephine's *Madame Argent* could have adorned herself with any name in the world.

"And the other one?" he asked Norton. The second woman was lithe, and once probably quite regal with sharp features with long hair. Matted and tangled with sea water now, her hair showed signs of the glorious color of autumn honey.

"Madame du Tourneville."

Two women, one perhaps five years older than the other. One silver-haired duchess, one golden. One with an honorific, one with a specific name.

"Had you ever seen them before you saw them on board?" Russ asked her, his gaze upon the two on the floor.

"Never." Mrs. Norton took another swallow of her wine. "You have stew? I'd like some, if I may. When they came before with food, I could not rally to eat."

Josephine nodded. "Of course. Do you know how they

fare? Have they been awake or talking when you've been awake?"

"That one, yes." She pointed to the golden-haired woman.

Madame du Tourneville, the younger of the two women on the floor, stirred and pushed herself to sitting position against the wall. Bleary-eyed, she cleared her throat. "I'd like to eat too, *s'il vous plaît.*"

"Of course." Russ noted her English was good, but tinged with French pronunciation. He held a bowl while Brewster's daughter scooped stew for her and Mrs. Norton. When the pot and pitcher were empty, he dismissed the two Brewster girls. "We'll take care of them here. You should go and help your parents."

The two castaways ate and drank with more eagerness than they should have. After a few minutes, both struggled with swallowing and coughing.

At long last, Madame du Tourneville surrendered to her infirmities and sank against the wall. Her hand lax upon her spoon, she sighed. "Who are you?" she asked Josephine and Russ. "Not..not...*propriétaire, non?*"

Russ introduced himself and Josephine to her. "And you are?"

"Madame du Tourneville. Cousin to Madame la Duchesse de Saint-Aubin."

"And this is she?" Josephine gestured toward the other lady upon the floor.

The young woman nodded, listless. "I have served her for many years. She wished to leave now that the Bonapartes return. We are a family originally from the Gironde, never trusted by royalists or imperialists alike."

"Do they rise again now against Napoleon's return?" he asked. Since the Terror, those in the Gironde near Bordeaux had fought against any who tried to rule them. Any news of their rebellion would be welcome in Whitehall to those who hoped that Frenchmen rose *en masse* against the returning Corsican.

"They do. Unhappy as ever," Tourneville told him with bitter resignation.

Josephine took the cups from both ladies. "Rest now. I will return later and bring you more to eat and drink."

Later as she and her husband took the stairs down to seek their own supper, she worried. "We may never know if any of those three are our *Madame*."

"But wonderful of you to remember Mrs. Norton."

"Papa speaks of her and her husband often. He lost track of them after the Treaty of Amiens ended." That temporary peace between Napoleon and Britain began in eighteen-o-two and lasted barely more than one year. "When Papa heard nothing, he wondered if they'd been swept up by the French police and he was very sad. I know that Mr. Norton was part of Papa's network."

"Bears asking her about her past. But for now, we will eat." He curled his arm around his wife's waist and led her to the bar room. "Later, we will return. Perhaps with time and sustenance, they all will feel better and we may learn more."

CHAPTER 8

$\mathcal{O}$ ver their own bowl of stew and wine, Russ and she made acquaintance of a few among the many stranded travelers. From them they learned that all roads to the inn were now closed. One woman talked of seeing a land slide and escaping its force just in time.

The owner of the inn, Mister Brewster, said the high tide would come in early at three or four in the morning. "I pray it does not come so far up the shore that we are endangered."

"Has it ever?" Russ asked him.

"My father said in the eighties, it took out a few cottages on the shore."

"But not the inn?" Russ added.

"No, milord. Not us. We've been here since old Queen Bess. Hope to stay until eternity, too."

The travelers appeared to be strained, trying to do their best to ignore the virulence of the storm. Talking easily with others, making new acquaintances, each seemed cheerful.

Russ recognized no one among the travelers. Josephine, however, spied a lady across the room, whom she'd met years ago at school. She told him she'd like to renew their acquaintance and took him with her to introduce him. Josephine's father often said she had never met a stranger in her life…but tonight, amid the attempt at conviviality in the gathering room, she worried that indeed she had. Both Mrs. Norton and Madame de Saint-Aubin had secretive natures and she could not yet fathom what each concealed. Yet she had to learn.

Though she wished to deny it, the storm added to her dismay, a downpour that beat upon the roof of the old inn and brought even more rain-soaked travelers in from the blustery shore. Lightning crashed and thunder drummed in tune with it. She pressed close to her new husband for warmth and comfort.

He circled an arm around her shoulders and took one hand in his. "My God, you are freezing. We must get you more wine and a hot brick to take up to our bed."

"Oh, no. Please. I will not be a bother to the owner and his family. There are so many here to cater to. Besides, my hands and feet are always cold. Comes of being born in August, I believe."

But he did not laugh. "Let's finish our meal and go up, shall we?"

Much later, they climbed the stairs to their room. Her little dog Rose scampered close behind them.

"I'm eager to return to our castaways," she confided in Russ as he closed their door upon them.

"I see it in your eyes."

"Forgive me, won't you?"

He led her to sit upon the bed and cast his gaze down as he toyed with her fingers. "Josephine, you need never ask to do as you must and leave me—"

He sounded so practical that her heart ached.

"I am not so sensitive as that, because I trust you, my darling."

She put two fingers to his lips. "But we have not had the usual wedding and honeymoon. I left you for business."

He splayed his fingers into her hair and cupped her throat. "As did I, sweet lady."

"Still in all. Dear me, Russ. I want us to be one but—"

"But tonight is not the time for that. You have suspicions of that woman, Norton. I don't blame you. The other woman does not seem blameless, either. And you must learn more." He raised her hand and kissed the back. His mouth was firm and oh so inviting. "There will be a better time. Soon. I want that to be joyous for you."

"And for you," she added with an urgency to convince him.

"Trust me, will you? To be with you as your true love will be the most divine experience of my life. I pray to make it yours."

"Oh, Russ..." She surged toward him and kissed his cheek. "You are so good to me."

"A mere reciprocation for your generosity to me and to all others."

"You are too complimentary."

"Ah, but you are mine to compliment as I wish as often as I wish."

She tipped her head to and fro, a grin upon her face. "I shall indulge myself in that."

He paused, his expression a ripe declaration of his need. "Then I will continue to pamper you. Now," he said and pulled back to gaze down at her attire, "why not wash your face and hands then change your gown? I will serve as maid. Good training, don't you think for the future? And then we shall go down and get one of the Brewster girls to fetch us more wine for the injured in the far chamber."

After she had washed her face and hands and brushed out

her hair, she tried to pin it up. "I'm not good at this," she said jabbing pins into the heavy mass.

"Let me help." He took a few pins from her and with surprising dexterity, created a French roll that was tidy but sat heavy at her nape.

"You are skilled at this, dear sir."

"Now who compliments too much?"

She turned and hugged him close. How she hated to leave him.

"I don't approve of you tiring yourself out," he said at last and put her from him. "You've had a long day and I want you to return as soon as you think them settled."

She nodded. "I will do that."

"Though we won't be spending the night as once we intended, my wife, I do want to warm your fingers." His bright eyes danced in mischief. "I also have a special technique to bring blood to cold toes."

She threw back her head and questioned him with a teasing glance. "You apply hot compresses?"

He barked in laughter and crushed her close. "I apply hot kisses."

Her mouth fell open. "In that case, I will be quick."

He locked his wicked gaze on hers. "You do that."

Josephine hurried down the winding corridor and up the back stairs with a candle in one hand, more in her pockets and her jug of wine in the other. Rose followed, her tail wagging. Josephine paused and in the dim light found Mrs. Norton stretched out asleep, but Madame du Tourneville leaning over the body of the Duchesse de Saint-Aubin. She appeared to be putting something around her throat, but Josephine could not see what it was. As Josephine gained the top of the stairs, the woman fell back. She'd been securing the blanket around the duchess's neck.

"Ah, *vin*," she sighed and threw Josephine a tight smile. *"Je vous remercie."*

"How is *Madame la Duchesse?*"

She shrugged. *"Le même."*

The same. Not good. Josephine poured wine for her and waited until she seemed comfortable before handing over the cup. The duchess opened her eyes wide and suddenly, she seemed restless and on alert. Mrs. Norton, however, slept with her mouth open. She also snored.

Josephine sat down between Madame du Tourneville and the duchess. How was she to learn more about the two women's loyalties? The younger woman's previous statement that they were from the Gironde told Josephine little of their recent lives. "You and the duchess are of the old regime. Did you return to France when Louis was reinstated last spring?"

"A long story. From the first, the Duchess de Saint-Aubin and all her family sided with the republicans. She remained faithful. Always. The result? Ah, well. Bonaparte allowed *Madame* her chateau. Her land, her jewels." Her tone held respect but also resentment.

Why? "Did the duchess like the emperor?"

The woman rolled a shoulder. "What is to like, eh? Any man with all power eventually becomes an animal."

"Do you imply she did not appreciate all he did for France?"

The woman scoffed. "You could say that, *oui*. She appeared to support him *carte blanche*. Nonetheless, in the past weeks Fouché sought her out."

Joseph Fouché was Napoleon's Minister of Police, a ruthless fellow who changed sides as often as his Minister of State, Talleyrand. "What did he do?"

"Tried to turn us. Took away her son."

"No!"

"Sent him to Vincennes."

The old fort east of Paris had held hundreds of French prisoners over the centuries. Most never saw freedom again. "And?"

"He escaped, but she knows not where. Two weeks ago, her chateau was attacked by mobs and burnt to the ground. Fouché instigated it. If they'd caught her, they'd have carted her off to Vincennes, too, we are certain."

So Madame la Duchesse de Satin-Aubin might very well be her *Madame Argent*. Well placed to know much about the court. Smart enough to survive all these years as an agent of the British. Wise enough to leave Paris when those in power in the Empire turned against her.

Time to learn how they escaped. "Tell me, *Madame*, about how you were able to survive the ship wreck."

"I cannot remember much. The storm, the wind, the rain, it was…" She circled a hand in the air. "Terrible. I was so…so afraid. We two clung together. So very afraid." Her words came slowly as she relived the moments that showed as horror on her ashen face. "We fell together against others as the ship tossed. This way and that, it went. Out there? Now?" Her dark eyes went round with fear as the sounds of waves crashing upon the shore rent the air. "It is the same, *oui?*"

"Catastrophic. The proprietor says high tide begins to come in over the night. The storm does not stop but builds." Yet Josephine wanted to bring her some hope and comfort. "Are you warm enough? Do you wish for anything?"

"No, *merci*," said Madame du Tourneville.

"Blankets," murmured the duchess.

Happy to hear her voice, Josephine turned to the lady who stared up at her with clear blue eyes. "*Madame la Duchesse*, you are awake."

"No!" snapped her companion. "She has the temperature. She is not well."

But the duchess reached out to Josephine, her long fingers plucking at her like talons of desperation. "*Madame* Stanton— but—but not?"

Why would she ask that? Josephine grasped her hand in comfort. Only if the duchess had overheard Mrs. Norton proclaim she knew her as Josephine Meadows would she wonder about her identity.

"Madam Stanton, *oui*, I am. But a new bride. Formerly Josephine Meadows of Meadows Trading Company." Did her lashes flutter at mention of the company? "I am here to help you get to London. That is, if you wish to go. Do you?"

She crooked a finger at Josephine to beckon her closer. Licking her lips, she tried to speak. "I am…"

Josephine bent close, afraid she might speak too loudly any words that might harm her. "*Oui, Madame.* What is it you want?"

"Water."

Relief swamped Josephine. "I have wine at the moment. Would you like—?"

"*Vin.*" The duchess gripped Josephine's hand. "*Oui.*"

"Yes, that I can get for you. And another blanket." She glanced around. She didn't know where or how, but she would give the lady her own if she could find no other. "What else?"

The duchess tugged on her sleeve.

And Josephine bent closer.

"Laaaal," was all she could gather from the lady's lips. She stared at Josephine and shook her head once. Then crooked a finger at her again.

This time, Josephine leaned so close, she could feel the duchess's breath on her ear.

"Lille."

This was a city in northern France, a garrison held by the French. Not far from Brussels. How it was provisioned with soldiers, ammunition and food was of prime interest to the Allies of the British. *Madame Argent* had often before sent news of the garrison's strength through the Meadows Company network. Josephine needed the duchess to continue now.

The lady licked her lips. *"Vin, s'il vous plaît."*

"She's awake?" Mrs. Norton struggled up on one elbow.

Madame du Tourneville fretted.

"No, no," Mrs. Norton said, "I will get it."

"Stay where you are." Josephine shot to her feet. "Both of you, please." She fetched the jug and a cup, poured and returned to sit down at the side of the duchess.

The woman drank eagerly, but a slide of her eyes told Josephine that she noticed the other two women were up and about. The duchess sank to her bed of hay, squeezed shut her eyes and alas, it appeared, would say no more.

Was the duchess wary of her two female companions? If so, why? Was this woman her *Madame Argent*?

"Sleep, all of you. I will remain." She should go down to tell Russ about her decision and her speculations about the two women here. But the eeriness of the storm and her suspicions combined into justifications to remain where she was. He'd told her to use her best judgment. She would. She picked up a blanket from a neatly folded pile upon one trestle and tucked it up about the duchess. "There. Warmer?"

The lady blinked once. "Lille," she mouthed.

Josephine lifted her forefinger to ask for a moment.

The duchess widened her eyes in recognition, then laid down her hand upon the back of Josephine's with five fingers spread. Then she picked up her hand and laid it down on Josephine's with four fingers out.

"Nine?" Josephine mouthed.

One nod.

"Soldiers?" she silently asked.

One nod.

Nine thousand French soldiers in the garrison at Lille. While Wellington currently had thirty thousand assembling south of Brussels.

She smiled down at the duchess and continued to fuss about her with the blanket. "Do sleep now and rest. We are happy here, safe and warm. The storm will subside soon and all will be well."

Her duchess closed her eyes, a serene smile curving her lips. Mrs. Norton finished drinking her wine and returned to her makeshift bedding. Madame du Tourneville sat up, staring at her friend the duchess and at Josephine.

But Josephine not only was relieved but also desperately tired. She settled into a mound of warm hay herself, Rose next to her, and wrapped her wool shawl tightly around her. "Awaken me," she said to all, "if you wish anything."

The storm raged outside. Thunder rattled the old panes in the windows and drummed upon the roof. Josephine tossed and turned away from the others toward the wall. Curling into a ball for warmth, she smiled to herself. Tonight as the previous two since her wedding, she should have been in a sweet hot bed with her new husband. But she'd done her duty by everyone first. So had he. Comforting, he was. Her love. Soon to be her lover.

At last she let herself drift...

A thump pierced her slumber. She grumbled and turned. Rose growled.

Another thump shook the floorboards beneath her.

A cry, muffled and urgent, had her opening her eyes. The

candles had died. The night was raw with whirring rain and earth-shaking thunder...

"Die, damn you!" A ragged whisper of anger had Josephine awake.

She shot up to her elbow.

Rose barked, fierce.

A figure was bent over the duchess.

At first glimpse, Josephine thought it was Madame du Tourneville. But no. No!

Mrs. Norton knelt beside *Madame* working, kneading, grunting.

"What are you doing?" Josephine scrambled up and lunged for her.

Norton shrugged her off, glaring at her, teeth clenched.

"Stop!" Josephine sprang again, grabbling bits of Nortorn's threadbare gown.

Norton pushed Josephine away and bore down on the duchess.

Josephine struggled to her feet and darted full force at Norton. The woman whirled on her, the duchess falling back, gasping as Norton clamped her long agile fingers around Josephine's throat.

She clawed at Norton's grip.

But the woman howled, savage, using her weight to force Josephine to the floor beneath her.

Norton was heavy but not agile—and Josephine summoned a great momentum and rolled her about.

"Stop!" A male voice.

Russ!

"Ahhh!" Norton let Josephine drop and whirled on him.

He thrust her to the floor.

She stumbled.

Staggered.

Would have fallen on top of Josephine but she rolled away in time.

Russ reached for Josephine, pulling her up as Madame du Tourneville leapt toward Norton.

But Norton backhanded the French woman and sent her to the floor. Then she scurried toward the stairs.

"Get her!" Madame du Tourneville shouted as she stumbled over hay and blankets.

But Norton ran, taking the wooden stairs in a run that pounded with each step.

"Sweetheart?" Russ held Josephine by the shoulders and examined every inch of her he could see.

"I'm well! She tried to hurt *Madame*."

Rose ran in circles, barking her distress.

"We must get her, Russ!" Whoever she was, friend or foe, and whatever she knew, the woman could die outside in that storm.

He nodded.

Josephine ran toward the stairs.

He followed.

As Josephine scrambled down to the first floor, she saw only the pale gown of Norton as she rushed out into the black void of the storm.

At the door, Russ shouted above the din. "Stay here!"

"I can't!"

He frowned at her but spun toward the shore and trotted off.

Out in the wind and the rain, Josephine ran after him, instantly soaked to her skin.

The night, so dark, so black, gave no light to any endeavor. Wherever Norton had gone, it would do her no good. Worse, Josephine feared for Russ. And she could not see a thing before her. Not even her hand.

"Russ! Russ!" She called.

She yelled.

The rain stung like needles. The wind howled and raged. Oh, she could not lose him when she had barely even won him.

"Russ!"

She staggered forward and a wall of surf hit her and knocked her down. Her mouth full of briny sea water, she retched and crawled toward the inn on the sand and rocks that cut her hands and her legs. The wave receded, the drag as powerful as the one that slammed her to the shore. High tide. It was coming in and if Russ did not see it, feel it, he could be dragged away. Away from her. Forever.

To the very devil with Norton. Her life. Her crime.

I want my husband.

"Russ!" she screamed so long, so hard she swore that God above could hear her.

Another roar grew louder, louder and she thought she saw a wall of water so tall three men could not equal it. She ran backwards. "Russ!"

A wave crashed before her and in its might, took her down to stones and sand that cut like a thousand knives. A hard shell of fear, she clawed backward on all fours like a crab.

No. No! She would not die here. Not like this.

She got to her feet and called for him again. "Russ! Russ!"

A vise clamped around her waist and bore her up, her toes dangling in mid air. The hell of nothingness became the mighty embrace of her husband who bonded her to his torso and walked like Goliath with her in his arms. She clung to him, frantic with joy.

Did it take him minutes or hours or eternities to carry her through the howling dervish of the storm far from the devouring waves? But he did! He did, fighting all odds. He brought her to the shelter of the inn and thrust open the heavy door with a kick to the bottom iron plate. He whirled inside, put her to the wall and stood, his chest heaving, his breath harsh as the wind.

"My darling," he rasped and put his icy hands to her cheeks. Rain matted his dark hair and poured over the stark planes of his handsome face. His worried eyes adored her as he brushed cold wet hanks of hair from her face. "You are safe. Well. Oh, Josephine, my darling. I love you. What would I have done if I lost you?"

He pressed a salty kiss of devotion to her lips.

And with his act and his words, he wiped away the trauma of the night and made her life perfection.

"You love me?" She wrapped her numb arms around his waist and admired the chivalry of this man whom she could not live without.

"I do. I have since first you laughed in your father's office at some silly joke about…God knows what."

"Oh, Russ." Tears leaked out of her eyes.

Her little dog Rose weaved between her legs and Russ's.

Her husband smiled sadly and brushed rain water from her forehead and tears from her cheeks. "Nothing to cry about now, my darling. You have saved that woman upstairs. You are a hero. I should have come sooner. I was remiss. But I wanted you to have your time. You are always so efficient. So dedicated." With each thought, he kissed her cheek or her nose or her lips and started then again. "I love you."

She shivered and let the tears continue, a silent declaration of delight and fear. "And Mrs. Norton?"

"That's her name?"

"It's what she told me."

"Ah. Well." He brought her close, put his chin to the crown of her head and rubbed her back with his huge strong hands. "I believe she stepped into the tide. She won't be back."

And even if the woman did survive, she would not find any place of sanctuary. She could not escape this shore. All roads were closed. And all people on this shore were stranded.

"Here's Brewster," Russ said and turned aside to speak with the owner of the inn.

In quick summary, he told him of one woman's rush into the hell of wind and rain and surf. "I'm taking my wife upstairs to warm her and comfort her."

Josephine had more to do though, especially for the duchess. "I'll change and then go upstairs to check on our patients myself. But if you could do that now, please for me, Mister Brewster? One of the women attacked another and I hope she was not hurt. I will come to see for myself in a few minutes."

The man agreed and hurried off.

"Forgive me for that," Josephine told her husband. "I am concerned."

"I understand. Come. We will both change and see to your castaways. I think you have more to tell me about them."

"You know me well, sir." She pushed back his drenched hair from his forehead. "I wish to tell you everything quickly and get to the business of being your wife."

"You take care of your castaways, my darling, and I will order up a hip bath and hot water."

"Delightful idea." She kissed his nose, his scar and his mouth. "And after our baths, I will take you up on your offer."

"Oh, what's that?"

"How soon you forget!" she chided him, shook her head and spun for the stairs to their room.

He caught her wrist. "What did I forget?"

"My cold toes, sir! They need attention!"

He chuckled and picked her up to whirl her around in his arms. "Hot kisses for your toes! Madam, every day of your life I shall kiss each inch of you!"

And by one o'clock that Saturday afternoon, the Countess of Stanton, Josephine Downey née Meadows rose up on her hands from the tiny—but very satisfactorily used—feather-bed and climbed atop the long majestic body of her naked husband to grin at him.

Their worries over, their two French ladies safe and healthy despite the attack of the other, the Stantons had adjourned to their room for rest and the enjoyment of each other that they had postponed.

She kissed his jaw and traced the firm expanse of his lips. "Now it is my turn, my husband, to savor each inch of you."

He ran an open palm from her throat to her silken shoulder, to her firm breast and then her sweetly rounded hip. "I adore you, Josephine. My world was dark before the moment I saw you laugh. Now you are the sun that lights up my universe."

He chuckled when her cheeks burned with his compliment.

"Does this mean, sir, you are ready for me to kiss your toes?"

He settled back, donned a foolish grin upon his face and flung his arms wide. "I am yours, Mrs. Downey."

She threw back her head to chuckle.

He hugged her close. "Have your way with me, my love."

And then she did.

EPILOGUE

June 22, 1815
16 St. James's Square, London

*A*s the Meadows' butler closed the front door upon the last of their guests, Josephine sank into the open arms of her husband and rested her head against his massive chest. "A glorious evening! Unmatched anywhere!"

Russ chuckled and squeezed her tightly in his warm embrace. "A rousing success as hostess of your first ball, my dear Countess."

"Ah." She looked up into his laughing blue eyes and shook her head. "T'was Henry Percy arriving with those three captured French Eagles and laying them at the feet of the Prince Regent that did it."

At about eleven-thirty that evening, General Wellington's aide had rushed into the home of Josephine's father during a dinner party. Straight from the Continent, Percy still wore his blood-stained uniform. Much of the *ton* was in attendance, Prinny included, all having accepted the invitation of William Meadows, his daughter, now the Countess of Stanton, and her new husband, the Earl. Her papa, whose health had improved lately, had wished to have the event at his home to that he could come, even if he had to appear in his new wheeled chair. But he relished the idea of entertaining those whom he knew and served so well.

Their one-hundred and fifty-two guests had come because gossip had it that the new Countess and her husband had contributed significantly to the war effort and, out of courtesy and some curiosity, they had discreetly decided to overlook the Countess's background in trade. Details of the Stantons' contribution were scant, of course. Secrets had to be kept, and justly so. But the trio had to be recognized, honored if you will, by Society's polite acknowledgement. The guests, like all others in Britain, anxiously waited for confirmation of hints about three days of armed conflict between the Allies and that horrid creature Bony. Numerous merchantmen and smugglers fresh from the coast had declared a battle had begun June sixteenth in a small town south of Brussels. Therefore many thought it wise to forget one's worries, if only for a few hours, to dine and drink and dance while one awaited word.

"Ha!" Josephine discarded her husband's compliment. "I, dear sir, had little to do with the joy of the evening. All credit goes to the man who led them in that fight and to the thousands of soldiers and their families who now will need our care and attention, more than our homage."

"Madam, hear me." He threaded his long fingers through her coiffure. "Without your skills and dedication, we would have lacked vital information to send to Brussels. I will not let you demure and ignore the praise that is yours alone."

"*Madame Argent* was more brave. *Madame du Tourneville* as well." Both ladies resided now in a manse in Truro, a gift of the Government for services rendered. There, last week,

Madame Argent welcomed her missing son, the Duc de Saint-Aubin, who joined her in retirement.

"And now we can rest from our worries about Bonaparte and about Mrs. Norton's identity."

"That woman was wily," Josephine agreed with a stern set of her teeth.

When Josephine and he had described Norton to her father, the man had deduced that person in the chamber at the Barque was the true Mrs. Norton's sister. Mrs Norton had a younger sibling whom she'd suspected of working with the French, but try as she might, she could never prove it.

"Whatever her game once was," Russ said, "she now lies at the bottom of the sea."

Josephine sighed and swayed against him in fatigue, her breasts in the thin silk of her ball gown abraded by the super fine of his formal black attire. She suspected she'd soon have good reason to tell him about an imminent arrival which he'd conclude was more exciting than the appearance of those three golden prizes of war.

He laughed, a jolly sound, then bent and swept her up into his arms. "How am I so fortunate to know you, Madam?"

"Because you are a wise man," she said as he climbed the marble staircase to her old bedroom that they used when occasionally they stayed the night. "But I do wish you were wiser and did not strain your back to carry me up all this way."

"You're tired," he said simply and stared straight ahead, undeterred by her jibe.

"I am, my love, but you must take care."

"I do." He smiled as he gained the second floor and headed for her former suite. "I take care of you."

At the door, he asked her to turn the knob and swing wide the door. Inside, he shut it and strode straight through to their bedroom. There, he set her to the bed and plucked pins from her hair, earrings from her lobes, and from her throat, the emerald and diamond necklace that had been one of his wedding gifts. As he worked, she unwound his cravat. On late nights like this since their return to London, she sent her maid Jane to her bed early, and he his valet to his. The newly wed Stantons—it became well known among their staff—often preferred to act as their own servants to each other, their joy in their intimacy a hallmark of the couple's love affair.

He urged her to her feet and she took the opportunity to kiss him. She adored the firmness of his lips, the way he swept his tongue inside her mouth to foretell of the ecstasies to come. Over the weeks they'd been one, she'd learned new and sensuous ways to thrill him and herself. Lingering kisses were just the beginning of hours of bliss spent in his arms. She took his frockcoat down his arms, his waistcoat too, then swept down his braces. "I wanted to kiss you tonight when Percy laid those eagles before the Prince."

He crushed her close and spoke on her mouth. "I saw your glance. I was tempted to run away with you up here."

She threw back her head to laugh. "You rogue."

"I confess I am that." He spun her about and made quick work of the laces on her gown. Then he pushed it to the floor. Nuzzling her neck, he circled his arms around her to cup her breasts. "Wanting you is the challenge of my days."

She chuckled as he turned her yet again toward him and went to plucking at her stays, her petticoat and her chemise. Then naked as God had made her, she flowed against him. "We have never restricted the time when we can come together."

"I find I need you at all hours." He smoothed his big hot hands over her shoulders and down to lift her breasts. They blossomed with heat and longing as he caressed her. She arched backward and sighed as he bent to suck one and then the other into the searing cavern of his mouth. "Oh, you are so very good at that."

"Practice makes perfect," he told her, his voice a dark summons to new delights.

"You are always perfect," she whispered. "You make my sun stand still."

He grinned at her reference to the work of Marvell that they both adored. "You are my sun, my moon, my stars, my heaven on earth."

"Russell Downey, may you ever think so."

"Lie down, madam. I shall prove it."

Hours later, he rose from their rumpled bed, his wife asleep, sprawled in elegant repose, her long red tresses gleaming silver upon the pillows in the moonlight. Fulfilled and unimaginably happy, he went to view the sky through the windows to the garden.

Outside, the night lay before him, a spectrum of blues with nary a cloud obscuring the perfection. That was how he viewed his new life with his new wife. A clear firmament electrified by the bright colors of erotic delights, set to the music of his wife's laughter and her love.

And soon, if nature developed as it should, she would bring him more to grace the rhythm of their days and the harmony of their nights. She had not had any of her monthly courses since they'd married. He knew because they had enjoyed each other every day and night since that morning they first joined amid the storm in the old Queen's Barque Inn upon the Norfolk coast.

He could laugh at life now. She'd taught him how. Led the way, actually. Where once he had little faith in the future, she affirmed it would be bountiful—and he believed. Where once he doubted his choices in the ways of mating and affections, she had swept into his life with her verve and her devotion to everything and everyone she adored—and he followed.

Where once he had worried that he must never again marry, she had smiled at him and he had fallen irrevocably in love with her. Then when he had feared he might again wed and make a poor choice, she had shown him that to love her was no mistake.

He smiled to himself and turned back for his bed and his wife and the beauty of his days to come. In truth, this time, he had married at leisure—and he would enjoy her at leisure for the rest of his life.

THE END

A LITTLE PRAISE FOR LORD STANTON'S SHOCKING SEASIDE HONEYMOON

"A sweet romance between two mature adults in the middle of a storm where many lives are in jeopardy. Josephine is a strong-willed heroine who'll do anything to protect those she loves. The historical accuracy is impressive and adds depth to the story. This is my first time reading Cerise DeLand and it won't be my last. I got swept away with this one. **5 stars.**

N.N. Light's Book Heaven

TRAVELS WITH CERISE!

A FEW NOTES ON RESEARCH!

Lord and Lady Stanton's romance represents the essence of what I write in every novel. Solid historical fact about a specific slice of history is my *metier*.

Here, a storm in the Channel which actually occurred on these dates tells a larger story of ships and troops lost at sea. So too the preparations for defeat of Napoleon and the last scene where the *aide de camp* to Wellington presents the Prince Regent with the captured French Eagles are facts adapted slightly by me to fit the characters of this novel.

I hope you enjoyed the love affair between Josephine and Russell and that you will read many more of my novels available everywhere.

Do visit http://cerisedeland.com

WHO IS CERISE DELAND?

Cerise DeLand, aka Jo-Ann Power

Cerise DeLand, a USA TODAY Bestselling author, loves to write about dashing heroes and the sassy women they adore. Whether she's penning historical romances or contemporaries, she has received praise for her poetic elegance and accuracy of detail.

An award-winning author of more than 50 novels, she's been published since 1991 by Pocket Books, St. Martin's Press, Kensington and independent presses. Her books have been monthly selections of the Doubleday Book Club and the Mystery Guild. Plus she's won nominations and awards for Best Historical of the Year, Best Regency and scores of rave reviews from *Romantic Times, Affair de Coeur, Publisher's Weekly* and more.

To research, she's dived into the oldest texts and dustiest library shelves. She's also traveled abroad, trusty notebook and pen in hand, to visit the chateaux and country homes she loves to people with her own imaginary characters.

And at home every day? She loves to cook, hates to dust, goes swimming at least once a week and tries (desperately) to grow vegetables in her arid backyard in south Texas!

ALSO BY CERISE DELAND

Regencies

Naughty Ladies Series:

Lady, Be Wanton, #1

Lady, Behave, #2

Lady, No More, #3

Lady, You're Mine, #4

The Lyon's Den novels:

The Lyon's Share

The Lyon's Perfect Mate, Coming July 2023

Daring Belles Series:

The Raven's Last Bet, #1 with Bonus Book #2, Lord Stanton's
Shocking Seaside Honeymoon

Regency Romp Series:

Lady Varney's Risque Business, #1

Rendezvous with a Duke, #2

Masquerade with a Marquess, #3

Regency Romps, box set of #1-#3

Interlude with a Baron, #4

Christmas Belles, Romantic Comedy Series:

The Earl's Wagered Bride, #1

The Viscount's Only Love, #2

The Duke's Impetuous Darling, #3

The Marquess's Final Fling, #4

The Butler's Forbidden Fancy, #5

Aunt Gertrude's Red Hot Christmas Beau, #6

Christmas Belles Box Set, Books 1-6

Four Weddings and a Frolic, Romantic Comedy Series:

Lady Fiona's Tall, Dark Folly, #1

Lady Mary's May Day Mischief, #2

Miss Harvey's Horribly Lovable Fiancé, #3

Lady Willa's Divinely Wicked Vicar, #4

Miss Weaver's Last Handsome Frolic, #5

Delightful Doings in Dudley Crescent, Romantic Comedy Series:

Her Beguiling Butler, #1

His Tempting Governess, #2

His Naughty Maid, #3

Her Magnificent Stableboy, #4, 2023

Her Tantalizing Gardener, #5, 2024

Aunt Diana's Delectable Christmas Cook, #6, 2024

Regencies, Stand alone novels

Lady Starling's Stockings

The Stanhope Challenge, Regency Quartet, box set

Storm & Shelter, A Bluestocking Belles Collection box set

***

Victorian Romances

Those Notorious Americans Series:

Wild Lily, #1

Daring Widow, #2

Sweet Siren, #3

Scandalous Heiress, #4

Ravishing Camille, #5

If You Were the Only Girl in the World, #6

* * *

Military Romances

7 Brides for 7 SEALs Series:

You Were Always Mine, #1

No Getting Over You, #2

SEALs Going Hot, box set

Burning for Nero

Conquering Zeus

Contemporaries

Is That a Gun in Your Pocket? (erotic comedic suspense)

Tall, Hard and Trouble, box set

***

Sign up for Cerise's newsletter: Cerise's Bon Bons